STELLA KON was born in Edinburgh and lived many years in Malaysia. The Singaporean playwright, novelist, short story writer and poet is best known for her play *Emily of Emerald Hill*, arguably Singapore's most performed play. Since it was first staged in 1984, it has been produced by many directors numerous times in Singapore, Malaysia and at arts festivals in Hong Kong, Australia, New York, Hamburg, Berlin and Munich.

Kon is a three-time winner of the National Playwriting Competition and a Singapore Literature Prize Merit Award winner for her novel, *Eston*. In 2008 she won the Southeast Asian Writers Award. Her works have been studied in local and foreign universities and her latest interest is in writing musicals. Her paternal great-grandfather was Dr. Lim Boon Keng. On her mother's side she is a seventh-generation descendant of Tan Tock Seng. More information about the writer can be found on her website www.emilyofemeraldhill.com

OTHER BOOKS IN THE SINGAPORE CLASSICS SERIES

*Scorpion Orchid* by Lloyd Fernando

*The Immolation* by Goh Poh Seng

*Glass Cathedral* by Andrew Koh

*The Adventures of Holden Heng* by Robert Yeo

# THE SCHOLAR AND THE DRAGON

STELLA KON

EPIGRAM BOOKS / SINGAPORE

Copyright © 2011 by Stella Kon

Introduction copyright © 2011 by Kirpal Singh

All rights reserved. Published in Singapore by Epigram Books.
www.epigrambooks.sg

*The Scholar and the Dragon* was first published by
Federal Publications in 1986

Cover design & book layout by Stefany
Cover illustration © 2011 by Lester Lee

Published with the support of

National Library Board Singapore
Cataloguing-in-Publication Data

Kon, S. (Stella)
The Scholar and the Dragon / Stella Kon.
– Singapore : Epigram Books, 2011.
p. cm.
ISBN : 978-981-08-9931-8 (pbk.)

I. Title.

PR9570.S53
S823 -- dc22   OCN747759568

This is a work of fiction. Names, characters, places, and incidents either are the product
of the author's imagination or are used fictitiously. Any resemblance to actual persons,
living or dead, is entirely coincidental.

10 9 8 7 6 5 4 3 2 1

To the memory of
Dr. Lim Boon Keng, 1869-1957

## Introduction by Dr. Kirpal Singh

I want to begin by quoting from a text message sent to me on 23 August 2011 by the author of this remarkable book: "I will feel happy if the story can bring the great pioneers of early Singapore to life in the imaginations of Singaporeans today." In a follow-up text message, Stella Kon said, "I ain't a historian."

Both of these texts from our dear author highlight an interesting issue which has been debated and discussed for centuries: when is fiction also history? I assume that most readers will be familiar with historical fiction—that species of fiction which, contextually, has a specific historic setting. Fiction as history, though, is a little more complex and complicated—in such a genre, the author, like Kon, wants to educate readers primarily about the history of a nation, a community, a people, rather than use history purely as a setting to provide a dramatic interplay between and among characters. The distinction is a fine one and not easily grasped or understood; this notwithstanding, it does pose a real challenge to readers who prefer to think of fiction simply as fiction—that is, an imaginative work bearing little or no resemblance to people living or dead. In Kon's text messages we discern an uncomfortable attempt at trying to stay balanced: Kon wants to both re-present history while at the same time insisting that she is not a historian. Much of our delight in reading *The Scholar and the Dragon* comes, therefore, in our own glimpses of recognition (did we not read about that character somewhere in our history texts?) as well as in our relishing of the quaint customs, practices and traditions of a bygone era (to think that even here in little, colonial Singapore, Chinese men wore long pig tails as late as the early twentieth century.)

A second related point also needs to be both noted and appreciated. Our author, Stella Kon, is a descendant of one of the major characters in the book: Dr. Lim Boon Keng. Kon is his great-granddaughter and therefore, in the expressly spelt-out manner of the Confucian texts that constitute the background against which the different tensions between and among the characters unfold and locate, we sense a clear alignment of authorial perspectives. Fictional, or imaginative, bias is always taken as a given; but bias in a text claiming also to provide some sense of "real" history can often become suspect. It is reassuring thus to be told by Kon herself that in the dramatic conflict portrayed between Dr. Lim and Dr. Sun Yat Sen—or of their respective advocates and followers—sides, as such, are avoided so as not to mislead. In the spirit of narrative storytelling, truth to character does override truth to historic reality. Some may see this as odd, even paradoxical, but we do need to make such allowances if we are to enjoy the tale without being constantly interrupted by remembrances of historic realities.

As we go through the book we realise yet another dimension; again related to our author. Kon is essentially a writer of drama, which is to say, she is best when capturing and rendering conflict, especially conflict through dialogue. It does not come as a surprise to any reader who knows Kon's dramatic scripts that, so frequently, it is the "voices" of the characters which make the book entertaining and readable. Whether these voices are plain colloquialisms or direct imitations of received/accepted pronunciations and tonalities, they do give the characters a richness which otherwise would not be present. Take for instance, these lines which open the narrative:

"So this is Singapore city, boy!" said Boon Jin's uncle. "Very big, very modern! You have nothing like this in old China, eh?"

Boon Jin and his uncle stood on the deck of a P & O liner. Uncle waved across the harbour, at a skyline of white domes and spires and columns rising against green masses of jungle. "Nothing like China, eh?" Uncle repeated again.

"No Uncle," Boon Jin replied politely. He remembered the huge foreign buildings in Amoy city, where he had gone to school.

Didn't his uncle realise that China was rapidly entering the new age? But he listened respectfully to his elder relative, as a Confucian student should do.

"You will have to get used to modern ways Boon Jin!" his uncle continued. He looked at Boon Jin's hair, tied in a long tail down his back. "You're still wearing your queue, so old-fashioned! My son and his friends at the Anglo-Chinese School have all cut their hair in the Western style."

"I shall certainly do as you say Uncle, if my father approves," Boon Jin said.[1]

This somewhat dramatic opening scene of the book actually helps readers understand that what is going to follow will mostly be some kind of working out, some kind of balancing of perspective between the old ways and the new ways, between the older generation and the younger generation, between life in China and life in Singapore. Boon Jin is caught right in the centre of this potentially explosive situation. As he grows up and experiences more and more of the life in modern Singapore, he harks back to the old ways of living he knew in old China. History does not always repeat itself, despite claims to the contrary. What it often does is to help shape the present and future, if the major players so choose. *The Scholar and the*

*Dragon* quite exquisitely explores the many choices that we are either given or create for ourselves as we move places, homes, feelings and loyalties. As in the book so in our time now, people confront difficult decisions almost on a daily basis, wondering how they should act and respond, what would the consequences be if a wrong choice is made, a wrong decision taken.

Values and attitudes go beyond the individual, leaving the individual sometimes in quite dire straits, torn between commitment and loyalty. Our hero Boon Jin is shown to be in such situations a lot of the time and as he makes his choices and takes decisions, so his life changes, frequently transforming his orientations, to the surprise (on a few occasions, shock!) of those around him. The gifted storyteller (and Kon is certainly one such) knows how to cleverly weave the inherent contradictions of a changing society to convey deep, inlaid emotions that do not seem to want to go away. Individual conduct is measured against the conduct of the collective which forms the community in which the individual must live if he or she wants to flourish. We are living witnesses to these undercurrents of change as contemporary Singapore goes into the throes of trying to become a vital, global city. A hundred years or so ago, the likes of Boon Jin contended with the major shapers of history, the likes of Lim Boon Keng or Sun Yat Sen. These two men were giants in and of their time and one of the more intriguing aspects of our book is the way in which Kon deals with the obvious disagreements between these historically large figures. Dr. Lim Boon Keng, obviously the more westernised, was perhaps less given to revolutionary fervour than Dr. Sun Yat Sen, whose passion for homeland China in the end resulted in the Revolution of 1911 and set China on the path to progress and modernity. The debates surrounding the tremendous influence of these two men will, no doubt, continue and much might be revealed as time passes; but there is no gainsaying the fact that between them, these men determined the destiny of most of the overseas Chinese of their time. Both men were deeply admired for their knowledge and understanding of human beings, both had huge numbers of followers, both displayed extraordinary capacities for leadership and both left large legacies. It is to our author's credit that when we close the book we move away with deep impressions of and about these larger-than-life characters.

And so where does this leave our understanding, perhaps even our realisation, of the book's title: *The Scholar and the Dragon*? Who is the one and who the other? Or are we to appreciate that the book defies such simple (even simplistic) categorisations? Boon Jin's uncle's trusted employee belongs to an underworld gang which calls itself by some variant of the Dragon's name. My own sense is that while it is clear that the "scholar" appellation might easily be applied to someone like Boon Jin, the "dragon" appellation is more of a "tease".

If I am right, the "dragon" image/metaphor is multi-layered (the "scholar" image/metaphor is not): and hence the term "dragon" may be used to describe men of multiple capabilities. From this perspective, several of the characters in the book may be termed "dragons" without too much inaccuracy or fault. However, the label "scholar" has to be much more judiciously applied because it conveys and stresses the qualities of knowledge, understanding and wisdom. It is Boon Jin who is constantly thinking about his classical education with its overlay of Confucian thought and admonitions and it is he who is most conflicted in the book's narrative. As readers will observe, every chapter of the book begins with an epigraph, some sagely saying which is, supposedly, known to all who belong to the Chinese culture. Of course, it is also to be stressed that unlike China, the modern city of Singapore (even a hundred years ago) was already diverse with many British, Malays, Indians and Eurasians living side by side with the majority Chinese. Chapter Twelve of the book contains the following epigraph:

> Man from his beginning was virtuous,
> Later corrupted by evil influence.
> By studying the Classic Books
> Inborn morality may be restored.[2]

The lines, the author tells us, are attributed to Lu Xiang

Shan of the 16th century. I did some research and found that the name is chiefly linked to a neo-Confucian philosopher of the twelfth century but whose ideas were forgotten for a long time till championed by another scholar-philosopher in the sixteenth or seventeenth century. So we do have to be cautious as we try to negotiate our way between and among the varied philosophies presented throughout the book we are reading. Lu attempted to be "universal", offering humanity a way of looking at itself so as to become better, more civilised and more developed as moral, sentient beings. Not everyone fully comprehends the finer aspects of such a doctrine but I am assuming most readers will know enough to follow the thinking behind the epigraph: that through the reading of good books we can become more moral. This standpoint is, naturally, provocative and we must leave it to each reader to decipher and decide whether the embedded meaning(s) hold in today's perplexing world.

• • •

And so I return to the book's title once more. Boon Jin fights a long, often lonely struggle to reach somewhere, to become someone. His story is not atypical; many a newcomer, migrant, learns painfully how best to manoeuvre and make good. Ultimately life is a promise with several bids and it is not always that the highest bid(der) wins. We see in the book how everyone seems to evolve, grow up, mature—and perhaps none more so than the alluring Quek Choo, the sister of the man who is at once both Boon Jin's copy and also a kind of doppelganger. I shall leave readers to track and trace the fate and fortunes of this gifted young woman, growing up in a man's world but shrewd enough to recognise the vanity and frailties of the male ego. As expected, the book does end with our hero marrying the indefinable Quek Choo (who herself states that she does not quite fit into any of the categories which the men around her try to define her with) Modern in her thinking and behaviour (to the point where both her brother and her husband-to-be seem bothered) and robust in her articulations, Quek Choo reminds me of the many heroines in Chinese literature who enter the dodgy worlds of men, in disguise, and assume control and authority. Quek Choo may be said to be an early representative of the "nonya", the curious mix of Chinese and Malay which forms the ancestry of many illustrious Chinese families of modern Singapore—a kind of prototype for Kon's later Emily. Quek Choo might well be the "dragon" in disguise, breathing both fire and water, uniting mind with body and spirit. The mysteries of the dragon sometimes can escape the profound searching of the scholar.

*The Scholar and the Dragon* is a book which, once we start

reading, seems very reluctant to have us put it down before finishing. It does have what many call the "power to involve" readers. Each reader will take away different possible "lessons" from it (remember I do call the author an "educator") but in the end the majority of us will agree that here is a nice, good illustration of the way in which history can be turned into engaging fiction. For a generation that does not, apparently, want to have too much to do with history as a subject, such a book may well offer the means to enter a period which laid the seeds of current nationhood.

Dr. Kirpal Singh, 2011

**NOTES:**

1. Stella Kon, *The Scholar and the Dragon*, Epigram Books, Singapore, 2011, p. 1.
2. Ibid, p. 219.

# THE SCHOLAR
AND THE DRAGON

The historical events of this period are fully described in Dr. Yen Ching-Hwang's book *The Overseas Chinese and the 1911 Revolution*. This novel follows history very closely. However the names of several prominent Singaporeans who appear in it have been changed. For example, the house which I have called "Tintagel" is really the Sun Yat Sen Villa at Balestier Road, and Boon Jin, his friends and family are fictitious. Dr. Lim Boon Keng, the author's great-grandfather, is a real person who towered over his generation as he towers over this book.

—*Stella Kon*

On the sixtieth anniversary of the Wenguang Chinese Academy,
all concerned with the institution wish to pay tribute to
their founder Mr. Tan Boon Jin, the well-known Singapore
philanthropist and educator.

Mr. Tan was born in China in 1890 and came to Singapore at
an early age. He devoted much of the proceeds of his successful
business ventures to the cause of Chinese and English education in
Singapore. For many years he also contributed a regular column to
local Chinese newspapers. His essays and other writings have helped
to shape public opinion among the Overseas Chinese.

—*Commemorative volume of the sixtieth anniversary
of Wenguang Chinese Academy, Singapore, 1980*

# 1

> The migrant bird longs for the old wood
> The fish in the tank thinks of its native pool.
>
> —*Dao Chien, about 400 A.D.*

"So this is Singapore city, boy!" said Boon Jin's uncle. "Very big, very modern! You have nothing like this in old China, eh?"

Boon Jin and his uncle stood on the deck of a P & O liner. Uncle waved across the harbour, at a skyline of white domes and spires and columns rising against green masses of jungle. "Nothing like China, eh?" Uncle repeated again.

"No Uncle," Boon Jin replied politely. He remembered the huge foreign buildings in Amoy city, where he had gone to school. Didn't his uncle realise that China was rapidly entering the new age? But he listened respectfully to his elder relative, as a Confucian student should do.

"You will have to get used to modern ways Boon Jin!" his uncle continued. He looked at Boon Jin's hair, tied in a long tail down his back. "You're still wearing your queue, so old-fashioned! My son and his friends at the Anglo-Chinese

School have all cut their hair in the Western style."

"I shall certainly do as you say Uncle, if my father approves," Boon Jin said. This reply was a little too clever, because Boon Jin's father was extremely old-fashioned. He was descended from thirty generations of Confucian scholars, and you couldn't get any more old-fashioned than that. Any suggestion of queue-cutting would have infuriated him.

Uncle knew this perfectly well. He blew out his cheeks and pursed his lips. "Boon Jin, in his letter to me, your father says that you are wild and disobedient at home; you have displeased him, and grieved your mother. You have run with bad company, and spoiled your chances of getting a good government job. He has sent you to me so that you can learn something useful, and perhaps reform your way of life."

Uncle said this in his loud voice, not caring if anyone overheard his criticisms. Boon Jin listened, screwing up his eyes against the sun, staring at the bright city of Singapore.

It was the third of February, 1906. To Tan Boon Jin it was the second day of the second month in the thirty-first year of the Emperor Guang Xu. Boon Jin was sixteen years old. The only world he knew was the China shaped by Confucius, which the Chinese Emperors had ruled for three thousand years. He had no idea that six years from that day, the last of the Emperors would fall from his Dragon Throne.

Boon Jin only knew that it looked as though this strange

Southern Ocean country was going to be no better for him than China. However during the past weeks he had heard so many lectures on his bad character, that when Uncle stopped talking he could make the correct reply in soft tones.

"I have made grave mistakes, because of youth and ignorance. With a fortunate opportunity before me, I hope to amend."

Uncle seemed satisfied with this. He talked jovially as he led Boon Jin to a small boat. They were rowed through the harbour, which was crowded with many steam ships and sailing ships, European craft and Asian. They approached a large white terminal building jutting out into the sea; they clambered out of the boat, across a space of green water, and climbed up slippery steps to the pier. So Tan Boon Jin set foot in Singapore for the first time.

Boon Jin looked round as he mounted the steps, excited to be stepping onto foreign land, though he showed nothing on his face. There was a long shadowy hall, crowded with men of many races in exotic costumes. The strangest thing to Boon Jin was that the colours of their faces varied so much, some dark and some very pale. Their languages hummed around him as he followed Uncle through the crowds.

Beyond the pier Uncle's carriage waited, drawn by two stringy horses. Their driver was a dark-skinned man in a white tunic.

"Get in, get in. We'll go to the house," Uncle said. The carriage, after standing in the sun, was a hot leather-stinking oven. The shades were pulled down against the glare. Boon Jin could see little, and with his uncle watching he was not going to peer about. He sat back and listened to the sounds of wheels clattering and voices shouting. The hot air was thick with smells, of horse dung and human waste and river mud, and spices sizzling in oil.

The carriage stopped for a while; Boon Jin saw that it was beckoned on its way, by a tall dark man wearing a turban above a Western-style uniform.

"Is that a British soldier?" he asked.

"That's not a soldier; he belongs to the Englishmen's Police Force," Uncle replied.

"They have police? They have laws and justice here?" Boon Jin asked. He knew that this country was ruled by the British; it had not occurred to him that they would have set up a civilised structure of government, with magistrates and law and order. But his Uncle misunderstood why he asked the question.

"Listen, boy. Even though this land is beyond the Chinese Emperor's rule, don't think there is no law and order here. You must behave better than you did at home. You got into trouble with the police in Amoy! You should have been thrown into jail for running about with those rebellious students. You were lucky you were not arrested. You would have been a disgrace to your family and your father would have disowned you. Instead of disowning you, he has been so good to you! He has found you this opportunity to come to a new country, which is under a different law than the Emperor's, so that you can make a fresh start here. You should be most grateful to your father, Boon Jin, instead of thinking of being disobedient."

Boon Jin listened quietly as Uncle continued like this for most of the drive. Uncle's tirade was less impressive than the lectures that Boon Jin got from his father, full of quotations and classical allusions so that he felt as though thirty generations of Chinese scholars were all criticising him together.

. . .

Uncle lived in a row of rich merchants' houses in Neil Road. You can see those houses still, if Urban Renewal hasn't got them yet, with steps going up from the road to the two carved wooden door-leaves, over-hung by a little skirt of green roof-tiles. There are flower-patterned tiles halfway up the walls, and phoenixes moulded in plaster on the frontage; the tall windows are closed by long shutters with hinged wooden louvres; when they are open, they are protected by elaborately-carved wooden railings. The houses go three storeys up, and a long way back, ventilated by open airwells.

The house was not so very different from houses in Kim Chiam town, near Boon Jin's home in China. But the people were different, when Uncle introduced him to the ladies of the house. His mother had coached him, before he left home, who his relatives were and how he should address them. There was First Aunt who was this Uncle's wife, and Second and Third Aunts; an older, formidable one was the Eldest Great-Aunt. There was also a girl of about fourteen who stared at Boon Jin boldly. Boon Jin's sisters of the same age would have died of shyness, if they had been allowed to meet a strange man.

They all wore batik sarongs and lace kebayas, which seemed totally foreign to Boon Jin. Their feet were not bound. "How are you, my great-nephew?" Eldest Great-Aunt greeted Boon Jin kindly and he had a shock to see that her mouth seemed to be full of blood; she was chewing what he later knew as betel-nut.

Boon Jin spoke to the older women. He used literary language to make the formal compliments. "Honourable Great-Aunt, First Aunt, Second Aunt, Third Aunt. My estimable parents convey their felicitations and compliments through their unworthy son. My honoured father regrets his deprivation of your august company. Grieving for this separation, he invokes heaven: may you have auspicious fortune, prosperous affairs and a harmonious household: all felicity and amity attend you!"

The formal speech seemed to impress the ladies and Uncle nodded with satisfaction. Then they actually introduced the girl. "Boon Jin, this is your little cousin Poh Nam!"

"How are you? Did you have a good journey?" she said cheekily.

"The celestial winds were auspicious and benevolent," Boon Jin replied. She giggled, as though he had said something funny.

One of the Aunts showed Boon Jin to the room which he would share with his cousin, Hock Joo. He started unpacking his belongings, thinking about what he had seen of this Singapore family. The first thing he had noticed was the way they spoke. His own family at home spoke Hokkien dialect in the way of educated people, with many literary words and phrases. But the people in his Uncle's household spoke like ignorant people; they used simple, rough words which only servants and peasants used at home, and other words which weren't Chinese at all.

"Hullo!" A young man about his own age came in. He wore European clothes, leather shoes, Western hair-cut. "Boon Jin?" he asked, and added something Boon Jin did not understand.

"Good evening," Boon Jin said cautiously.

"I said, I am Hock Joo, your cousin. Don't you speak English? You're a real China-simpleton, aren't you!"

"I am delighted to make your acquaintance," Boon Jin said politely.

"You do talk funny!" Hock Joo laughed. Behind him his sister Poh Nam peeped round the door and giggled loudly.

"Delighted to make your acquaintance," she mocked. "Why

do you use such queer old-fashioned words? You're like an old monk, a temple beggar!" She gabbled something to her brother.

Boon Jin kept quiet, hiding his anger and his contempt for their ignorance. He said to himself, that he must always remember to speak to his cousins in the way he spoke to servants and peasants at home.

A midday meal was served. The food was oily and spicy. The old ladies ate with their fingers and the younger people ate with Western instruments. Conversation was mostly in Malay and English. Boon Jin's cousins ignored him, but the eldest Great-Aunt spoke to him in good Hokkien, asking the usual things about how his parents were, how things were at home.

"My honoured parents are very well," Boon Jin replied.

"Does your father still supervise his business at the weaving shop?"

"My honoured father is occupied with his literary work. He has little time to attend to business," Boon Jin answered. This was not entirely true. The cotton-weaving workshop was doing badly, and Boon Jin's father had little to do there. But he spent his leisure time in the town, not at his writing desk.

"Your father is a government official, isn't he?"

"My father was an assistant to the local Magistrate; but he retired when my eldest brother passed his government examinations and was appointed as a primary school headmaster."

"And your older sisters are married? So you are the youngest child! Your parents love you very much, eh? It must be difficult for your father to allow you to travel so far away from home. You should be grateful to him."

"Yes." Boon Jin looked down at the gaudy tiles. He never liked it when he was told that he should be very thankful to his father; and he felt guilty at resenting it.

Later Uncle brought Boon Jin to the centre of the family business, on the bank of the black, stenchy Singapore River. It was a large warehouse filled with tall piles of bulging sacks; amidst which were a battered desk, a shelf of ledgers, a clerk reading a newspaper, and a cat nursing two kittens.

"This is our warehouse where goods are stored. You are to start working here to keep the account books. You have not done such work before? You do not know how to keep the books? That's how much your fine education is worth then! Well we will not expect so much of you for a start. You will have to learn. Chua will teach you. Chua is my compradore. Chua, this is my young nephew, a scholar from the old country, come to learn how we make our living here!"

The man Chua was a typical Straits Chinese. He wore Western clothes in thick white cotton. His grey hair was cropped short. Through thick-lensed horn-rimmed spectacles he glanced sidelong at Boon Jin, and nodded and beamed at Uncle.

"A scholar, a scholar. Can he write characters? Of course he writes characters. He will write letters for your office. He will be most valuable to you."

"He is to learn to keep the books and handle the accounts," Uncle said.

"He will keep the books. He will handle the accounts. He will learn all the business! Perhaps he will take over the business one day, eh? Perhaps he will be the Master here one day!"

"Maybe, maybe," Uncle said, with a shrug and a smile.

・ ・ ・

Towards evening Uncle's household grew very excited. The whole family, old ladies included, got into carriages which drove into town and parked along the seafront Esplanade. Boon Jin gathered that they were going to watch a grand procession which had been organised in honour of a visiting British Prince: Arthur Connaught, Queen Victoria's third son.

As dark fell, brass band music approached. Large glowing lanterns came bobbing through the dusk, accompanied by men carrying flaming torches. On each lantern were painted portraits of Westerners: the Prime Minister of Britain and his senior ministers. Then with thudding drums and clashing cymbals came dancing dragons, twisting and turning all over the street. There were more lanterns and three pretty little girls dressed in splendid Chinese costume, their open carriage decked with flowers and with the yellow dragon flag of the Emperor of China.

There was a brass band belonging to the Chinese Volunteer Company in quasi-military uniforms; there were representatives of many Straits Chinese clubs and social organisations.

Boon Jin was amazed to see his cousin Hock Joo marching along among a group of youths, with his face painted black, wearing a straw hat and a striped blazer. He grinned and waved to his family. He was strumming a banjo and playing Dixieland. "That's Hock Joo's band," said an aunt proudly, "the Brighton Minstrels."

Boon Jin, new in Singapore, did not understand just what he was seeing: the Straits Chinese of the British Crown Colony of Singapore, demonstrating their loyalties along with their sense of themselves as a community with its own identity. They brought their great procession, mixing Western and Chinese cultures, to greet Prince Arthur Connaught, whose brother ruled the British Empire. Those pictures of Cabinet Ministers which led the procession represented the Parliament of Britain. They were symbols of democracy.

Walking in the middle of the procession, heading the Straits Chinese British Association, was a man in good Western clothes with a little black beard. Though less than forty, he walked with the self-assurance of a man well-respected by others. "Dr. Lim Boon Keng," Uncle told Boon Jin, as though everyone should know who Lim Boon Keng was.

Everyone in Singapore did know. Lim Boon Keng was the foremost leader of the Straits Chinese. He was carrying an engraved silver box, and when they reached Government House he would make a welcoming speech to Prince Arthur, and present him with the casket on behalf of all the Straits Chinese. It must have been he who devised those lanterns, which were a salute to Britain and to democracy.

Thus Boon Jin witnessed the harmonious meeting of different cultures and loyalties. The day when British influence would be thrown off was decades in the future. Much nearer in time was the day when the Nanyang Chinese would haul down the yellow dragon flag for ceremonial burning. The aristocratic Chinese consul in his Mandarin robes, now among the honoured guests at Government House, would find himself hiding in terror from bloodthirsty mobs. The Old China he represented—the world into which Boon Jin had been born—would be completely swept away.

# 2

> Three basic relationships:
>
> obligations of princes,
>
> obligations of subjects,
>
> obligations between men.
>
> Observing these produces
>
> father-son harmony,
>
> husband-wife accord.
>
> —*The Trimetrical Classic*

In the year 1276 A.D. an ancestor of Boon Jin's had been the Emperor's Chief Minister. Ever since then the Tan family had been among the scholar-gentlemen who helped to rule China. In each generation the sons studied the classics, passed the government examinations, and took jobs as government officials. Each was expected to serve the Emperor and bring honour to the Tan family.

When he was very small Boon Jin thought the Emperor in Peking was the same Emperor that his ancestor had served.

His mother laughed when he asked about this and told him, "This Emperor is called Guang Xu. He is twenty-five years old, and he became the Emperor when he was a small boy like you. His wise aunt, the Empress Dowager, helped him to rule. When he sat on the Imperial Throne she stayed close by behind a screen, and instructed him how to rule."

Boon Jin liked to think about the young Emperor as a boy like himself, in the big palace in Peking.

When he was a little older he was brought to his father in the writing room called the Jade Study and formally presented with his own writing brush and book, inkstone and ink: the "Four Treasures" of a Confucian scholar. He knelt before an altar, holding a stick of incense in his chubby hands, and made reverences to the Emperor, to Confucius and to his famous ancestor.

"You must study hard," his father told him. "You must pass the examinations so that you can go to Peking and see the Emperor, and perhaps he will make you Chief Minister like your great ancestor."

After this Boon Jin began studying the classic texts. He had lessons in the Jade Study with his brother Boon Huat, to get ready one day to take the government examination.

There were three sets of examinations. If one passed the first set of district examinations one went up to the provincial capital at Foochow; if one passed the provincial examinations, one went to Peking, and the ten top scholars from the Peking examinations submitted essays to be read by the Emperor himself. At each stage of the examinations, nine out of ten students would be eliminated and only one would go on; the higher he went, the higher official position and honour he would receive.

Boon Jin's great-grandfather had been one of those who succeeded at provincial level. When he came back triumphantly from Foochow, the governor of Amoy sponsored a big banquet in his honour. He was given a study allowance, and clothes and travelling expenses for his journey to take the next set of examinations in Peking. But he was not successful in Peking; he tried again every three years till he had failed eight times, and finally gave up and accepted a government position in Amoy.

Boon Jin was sure that his Eldest Brother would do at least as well as Great-Grandfather. Boon Jin heard Boon Huat discussing literary themes with their teacher, quoting the poets and improvising new verses. Boon Jin thought he must be the most brilliant student in the country.

Most of what Boon Huat discussed with the tutor was far over Boon Jin's head, but he heard one phrase repeated many times—"Eight-Legged Essay". He just about knew what an essay was. He imagined an important-looking scroll covered with flourishing calligraphy: it was stretched out flat like a table, and had four stout legs on each side like the legs of a table.

He asked his father about it. His father, who usually did not pay much attention to small children, was pleased with the question and happy to explain at some length.

Briefly, there was this literary essay which had to be written exactly according to a prescribed pattern. It was divided into eight paragraphs; the paragraphs were called "legs", just like "feet" in European verse.

There had to be two introductory paragraphs, the first one with two sentences and the second with three; then two central paragraphs on the main theme, then two sets of original verses—one short and one long—and two concluding paragraphs. The form was as strict as that, and what mattered was not what you said but how beautifully you said it. Good literary style and deep knowledge of the poets were what examiners wanted. Original thinking was not in demand.

Boon Jin's father explained the form of the Eight-Legged Essay and wanted his son to try it out. Boon Jin was too young for this, and the day ended with Father losing patience and cracking Boon Jin's hands with the heavy ruler.

That night Boon Jin dreamt he was being chased by an Eight-Legged Essay. The silk scroll was covered with black and vermilion characters: it was spread out like a table, it capered after Boon Jin on carved wooden legs and chased him along endless corridors. The black and red characters got up and waved thick little arms, shouting, "Naughty boy! Stupid boy!"

So Boon Jin was very interested when one day his father came into the Jade Study shouting, "Kang Yu Wei has abolished the Eight-Legged Essay!"

"What! It can't be!" the tutor said unbelievingly.

"That wily bastard has poisoned the Emperor's mind," said Father, who under stress used language unfit for a Confucian scholar. "Look at the Imperial decree. No more Eight-Legged Essay in government examinations, and a parcel of other so-called "Reforms"—government administration reorganised and turned upside down, devilish railroads and factories to be built—no end to those damned modernisations!"

"How could Old Buddha allow it?" said the tutor. Old Buddha was the Empress Dowager, the young Emperor's aunt who had ruled for him when he was small.

"What can she do to stop him? Since the Emperor came of age and started ruling for himself, he packed the Old Ancestor off into retirement, and now this devil Kang Yu Wei is his adviser, his teacher, his corrupting influence!"

Boon Jin was frightened by his father's angry voice—he knew that one must always speak of the Emperor with the greatest respect. He crept off to his mother and whined, "Mother—Father is so angry, Father is scolding the Emperor!"

"You shouldn't be listening to Father's talk," his mother said automatically. She thought it over and added, "I have told you that the Emperor is young, a boy. He had some bad friends who made him do things that he shouldn't do. A boy should not have naughty friends, he shouldn't mix with bad company, do you hear that Boon Jin?"

This attempt to modernise China was the Reform of 1898. It is also known as the Hundred Days' Reform, because unfortunately it only lasted that long. After about three months the Empress Dowager, the strong-willed former concubine of the previous Emperor, gathered her supporters and seized power again. She arrested the Emperor's friends, locked him into his palace, and gave out an Imperial Edict that the Emperor was sick and she was Regent again. Politicians switched loyalties or lost their lives. The Reforms of Kang Yu Wei were thrown out.

The Empress Dowager was back in the driver's seat and meant to stay there. She kept her nephew under house arrest for the next ten years; said he was obviously too immature to rule for himself and she had to rule in his stead.

She didn't manage to catch Kang Yu Wei; he got away, minutes ahead of the head-choppers, and escaped to Japan. And students went back to writing Eight-Legged Essays for the examinations.

Boon Jin's mother, remembering that he had shown unseemly interest in grown-up politics, took care to explain to him that the Emperor had been a naughty boy who disobeyed his elders: now the Empress Dowager, his wise old Aunt, had properly disciplined him, and she had set everything right.

Boon Jin went on with his young life. He remembered Kang Yu Wei's name: he thought that if Kang wanted to abolish the Eight-Legged Essay, he must be quite a good fellow after all.

. . .

Every day Boon Jin and his brother spent hours in the Jade Study, practising calligraphy, studying the Classic Books with their tutor, who was one of their father's cousins. Above them hung a large black and gold board, with four big characters on it. The great Chief Minister himself had written them there, and his calligraphy had then been carved and gilded: "Classic study, bright light".

Sometimes their father came in, more often he was out playing mahjong. Gambling is not recommended by Confucius, but Father played every day for high stakes, with his crony the local Magistrate. Father was an excellent scholar however. He could happily have sat down for a drinking party with Po Chu-I in the ninth century. They would have composed instant verses for each other, swapped beautiful specimens of calligraphy, and quoted the same Confucian classics, without much communication difficulty. The culture in which Boon Jin was being trained went back a very long way.

When Boon Jin was ten years old the trouble called the Boxer Rebellion swept China; but Kim Chiam district stayed peaceful. Boon Jin only understood that "bad rebels" were making trouble. His elders were completely confident that law and order would prevail. China had always known rebellions, rebellions had always been suppressed, and the age-old rule of the Emperors would continue.

True enough, after a couple of years the Boxer Rebellion was put down and the Empress Dowager, who had had to flee from Peking, was back on her Regent's throne. But she had received some nasty shocks, and she began to realise that China had to modernise. Over the next few years, she started to introduce many of the changes Kang Yu Wei's Reformers had wanted. Naturally, she presented them as her own ideas.

The changes in the educational system upset Boon Jin's family a lot. First the requirements for the government examinations were changed; the famous Eight-Legged Essay was scrapped again and replaced by something called "Current Affairs". A couple of years later, the whole system of government examinations was closed down.

Boon Huat was preparing for the government examinations the year that the examination syllabus was changed. "What's Current Affairs?" he asked worriedly. "What textbooks do we use? Where do we get the model essays to learn by heart?" He had to read newspapers carefully, and Father was disgusted:

"Newspapers! Trash! Time-wasting rubbish, not fit for a scholar! Full of articles written in atrocious style, on subjects that change from day to day!"

Boon Huat did not do well in the examinations. He was given only a small post as a teacher in a local school. Father decided that Boon Jin should start going to the Geok Pin Academy in Amoy, which prepared students for the government examinations. He insisted that Boon Jin continue to write Eight-Legged Essays with the family tutor at home. But when the government examination system was dismantled, Father really thought it was the end of the world that his family of scholars had lived in for so many generations. There was no more hope that any of his sons would earn a high government position like the revered ancestor. In this despairing mood, he sent Boon Jin off to try to improve his fortunes in the Nanyang.

There were other reasons too, why Boon Jin was sent away from home. Before we go back to Uncle's house in Neil Road, more must be said about the two years that Boon Jin spent in school in Amoy.

· · ·

One day Boon Jin told the Aunt whom he lived with in Amoy, "Auntie, I'll be back late today, I'm going to our study-group meeting." He did not tell his Aunt that it wasn't schoolwork they were studying.

After classes Boon Jin hurried to the hillside where the students were gathering. Below the hill he could see the big natural harbour which made Amoy Island, at the mouth of the Pearl River, the big market and jumping-off point for South Fukien. In the middle of the harbour among the shipping was the little island of Kulangsu. Nearer the school he could see the dockyards, thronged with Chinese labourers; among them flashed the white of Western sailors.

A boy called Teochew Hoon stood next to Boon Jin. "Look at the soldiers," he said, pointing. A line of little red figures with rifles on their shoulders marched along the docks and tramped onto one of the steamships. "Damned foreigners," muttered Teochew Hoon, and "Behaving as though they own the whole country," grumbled Boon Jin. Saying bitter things about foreigners was fashionable among the students.

"What is the meeting for?" Hoon asked. "Has something special happened?"

"Something happened in Shanghai," Boon Jin replied. "I heard that someone committed suicide…I don't know why."

"Fellow students!" an older student shouted, getting up onto a fence, waving a newspaper. "We have asked you to come to hear about the heroic sacrifice of a Chinese martyr! His name is Feng Xia Wei, a man who lived in the Philippine Islands.

He was angered by the American law that forbids Chinese to enter America. The American attitude is an insult to the dignity of our country. Feng could not tolerate their insolent behaviour. In front of the American Consul's house in Shanghai, this hero Feng took his own life as a mark of protest."

"Ahh," went up a sigh from the students.

"Feng left behind a letter, which he addressed to all Chinese citizens, all his dear countrymen, the sons of Han! He urges us to join the boycott against buying American goods. Remember the blood of Feng Xia Wei!" The students listened to Feng Xia Wei's letter being read out. They groaned with sorrow for Feng and roared with rage against the foreigners.

The Americans in Shanghai probably thought the fellow must be a madman, not a martyr, to cut his own throat for nothing; he was just crazy, to think he could hurt his enemies by killing himself. Maybe modern Singaporeans can understand, without entirely sympathising. But those Amoy students were emotionally moved and inspired when they heard about it. They resolved to aid the boycott. Brushes and paint were brought; Boon Jin and others with good calligraphy wrote slogans that they all suggested onto big posters.

"Don't buy American goods", "Struggle against foreign insults", "Expel foreign intruders" and getting very daring, one long blue banner that said "Exhort Qing to expel foreign invaders".

The posters were put up on walls around the town. An American clipper, with the Stars and Stripes fluttering above her folded sails, was being loaded in the harbour. Some students ran down to the dockside and harangued the labourers; presently they dropped their loads and refused to go on working. The American captain raved and swore in vain. A unit of the local Magistrate's police came along; the students ran one way and the workers another, leaving the boxes scattered on the wharf.

. . .

The next day a special assembly was called at school. The headmaster—nicknamed Old Eyebrows, for obvious reasons—lectured the students, in best Confucian style, on the reprehensible conduct of certain parties who had contributed to lawlessness and civil unrest in the town. Any culprits apprehended in future, while engaged in such disloyal and treasonable activity, would be summarily punished and expelled.

Behind Old Eyebrows on the school platform were displayed some of the posters—only the relatively mild ones, not for example the blue banner that said "Exhort Qing to expel foreign invaders". That last banner was the one which got anyone involved in the action labelled "treasonable and disloyal", because reading between the lines, it implied violent criticism of the Emperor.

Boon Jin's father would never have tolerated such criticism. To him China was still the great, self-sufficient Central Kingdom, ruled by the all-powerful Son of Heaven. But when Boon Jin started school in Amoy, he had learned that this classic picture was a hundred years out of date. China wasn't great, but being generally bullied by Western powers; and even the Emperor wasn't really Chinese.

The Qing dynasty were descendants of barbarians from Manchuria who conquered Peking in 1644, just yesterday by Chinese standards; and many people in the Southern regions had never really accepted them as the rulers of China. After the brilliant and capable rule of Emperor Chien Lung in the seventeenth century, the dynasty kept running downhill. Its last forty years were dominated by that amazing woman, the Empress Dowager. Due to her manipulations, the last three Qing Emperors ascended the Dragon Throne as children less than six years old.

Meanwhile the modern Western world was developing its muscles and barging into China to get a share of its legendary wealth. China was technologically backwards in comparison. She lost a Japanese war, a couple of English Wars, an Opium War and a French War; and any number of diplomatic arguments backed up by Western guns and armies. The Americans, British, Germans, French and Russians walked into China, took possession of large areas, set up their trading centres, kept soldiers in garrisons and gun boats on the rivers, and generally acted as though their grandfathers had bought the place; while Chinese going to Western countries were being treated like dirt. Feng Xia Wei killed himself because America didn't "give face" to China.

"Exhort Qing to expel foreign invaders" blamed the Qing Government for being too weak to keep out the foreigners. It could not maintain law and order. In the last sixty years, the starving peasants had rebelled several times—revolutions were fairly standard for China, with thousands slaughtered, tens of thousands homeless; and the government sent soldiers to crush the rebels, and did nothing about the poverty and social oppression which had triggered them.

So what worried Old Eyebrows was not just students getting involved in labour disputes. This agitation looked like part of a growing protest movement in South China, against the central Government in Peking. If Old Eyebrows didn't deal with it firmly it could cost him his job—or put his head on the chopping block.

• • •

The next time the students called a political meeting, there were other students who believed that they were helping their country by warning the authorities. The same student leader was speaking in a public square. Posters had been put up and a crowd of the Amoy people had gathered; they listened to the speaker declaiming, "China must be stronger! China must modernise in order to regain her pride!"

Suddenly a large company of the Magistrate's police rushed into the square. They rushed to arrest the speaker, knocking aside the people in their way. The speaker, not entirely naive, disappeared into the crowd like a fish into muddy water. The police started arresting anyone they could grab. They tore down the banners. Boon Jin was stupid enough to try to protect one banner on which he had spent a lot of time: he tugged at the man who was going to pull it down. The man knocked Boon Jin down with his wooden pole. Boon Jin went rolling dizzily over the stones.

"You're one of the rebels!" the policeman shouted. Boon Jin realised rather late that he was in trouble. He staggered up as the officer reached for him; he eluded the reaching fingers with the agility of a child in a school playground, and ran as hard as he could.

He was very frightened. He ran back to his aunt's house and packed a few books and clothes, and told her that the school was closed for a few weeks. He took the ferry boat back to the mainland and got a ride on a vegetable cart going back to Kim Chiam.

He told his father the same story, that school was closed because of riots in the city. He explained the huge bleeding lump on his head by a blow from a cricket ball, to which his mother replied at some length that she had never liked those rough games unsuitable for a gentleman.

Three days later, Father came home from one of his trips to town in a great rage. "Boon Jin! Magistrate Pu tells me that the police want to arrest you, for treason against the Emperor!"

Boon Jin's legs felt weak. "No Father! I didn't!"

"How did they get hold of your name! Were you involved in those student riots last week? You must have been there! That's how you got that bump on your head!"

"I—I was there—but I wasn't involved! I didn't do anything!" Boon Jin stammered. In truth, he did not really understand what was going on; it had been exciting to work with other students, and write the words they told him onto big posters.

"What business have you got to be mixing with revolutionary traitors?" Father shouted. "Our family has always been loyal to the great Emperor; your ancestor was Chief Minister, your grandfather was a Magistrate. Useless, unfilial, traitor! You want to disgrace your family, kill your parents! Go and fetch a strong stick from the woodpile."

Boon Jing got the worst beating of his life. When it was over, before he could crawl away to his room, he had to bow and say, "Thank you, Father, for teaching me." He lay in bed for two days to recover, wondering all the time whether the policemen would come to arrest him and take him away to be executed. He knew that the penalty for treason was death for the guilty person and all his family; Father had not been exaggerating when he said that he could get his parents killed.

But the police did not come. Powerful Magistrate Pu, Father's mahjong crony, deflected further inquiries and protected the family. Two weeks later Boon Jin went back to school.

Father of course did not like Boon Jin to return to Geok Pin Academy; but he felt there was no other choice. The school had to prepare Boon Jin for the government examinations, so that he could get a good government job and earn money for the family. Father had been playing more mahjong lately and now owed large sums to that kind, helpful Magistrate Pu.

Tan family's affairs were doing badly. They owned a hillside planted with cotton bushes; and village women were hired to weave cotton cloth on handlooms, in a little weaving-shed on the estate. The sale of the cloth was the family's main business. But over past years the price of cotton had fallen, and Father complained the town merchants would not pay a reasonable price for his cloth.

One day while Boon Jin was at home a pedlar came up to the house, somehow gained admission and spread his wares over the front courtyard. Mother could not resist buying a small piece of cloth, printed with little red golliwogs, for one of the babies.

Father came back from town and exploded into a rage, shouting at the bewildered women, driving out the pedlar. "You give money to those devils who are breaking our rice bowl!" he curtly snapped at Mother.

Mother retired to the ladies' apartments for a week. Out onto the rubbish heap went the gay piece of cotton, woven in Shanghai on foreign-owned machines, sold cheaper than the cloth from Chinese weavers. Father cursed the foreign manufacturers, and never thought of trying to improve his methods to compete with them.

. . .

Boon Jin went back to school, with stern warnings from Father to stay well clear of any revolutionary activities. The warnings only made it more exciting to join the clandestine political activity which throbbed through the whole school.

They furtively passed around the writings of Kang Yu Wei, the exiled Reformer. They smuggled in the latest copies of the newspaper which he and his friends published in Tokyo. Boon Jin, with ability developed in memorising Confucius chapter by chapter, learned by heart large sections of the clear, elegant prose of a Reformist writer called Liang Chi Chao.

Eagerly they read up on the political structures of England,

America and France. England had the oldest democracy and the "Mother of Parliaments". A Parliament—a group of elected commoners, telling the King what to do!—was a shocking idea, even a blasphemous one if your ruler was known as the Son of Heaven. But students like to play with shocking ideas.

France had slaughtered her kings; America had never had any. These two countries functioned as Republics, governed solely by the elected representatives of the people, with no sovereign rulers. And some people like Teochew Hoon said that China should be a Republic, should get rid of Emperors and rulers, by a violent bloody revolution like the one in France. But Teochew Hoon was a wild man anyway. His idol was a notorious character who went around starting up rebellions throughout Fukien and Canton provinces: a fiery-eyed devil called Sun Yat Sen.

Most of the students wanted something more like the English way. Throughout China, intellectuals were joining Kang Yu Wei's call for the Manchu Government, run by the Empress Dowager, to give China a political Constitution: that is, to set up rules and laws that would put the Emperor's limitless powers under some control. And they wanted that control to be exercised by the representatives of the people: a Parliament.

"Give China a Parliament!" was the slogan, which tried to bring democracy to the ancient Empire of China.

• • •

The Empress Dowager's government regarded this call for a Parliament as treason against the Emperor, and anyone who joined in was a rebel. Boon Jin managed to stay out of further trouble with the police, though he read newspapers and joined student discussions. But he knew he was already a marked man on Old Eyebrows' confidential lists.

He thought his best chance was to go to Nanking University for his higher studies, where he would be beyond Old Eyebrows' influence. He was studying hard to take his first district-level examinations, when in November of 1905 another edict came out from Peking. The Chinese examination system, which had lasted for two thousand years, was abolished overnight.

Boon Jin was glad he wasn't there to see Father's explosion, the day that he heard the news. Father sent for him to come home at once, and the atmosphere at home was very stormy. Father really thought it was the end of the world his ancestors had known. For the first time, Boon Jin heard him criticise the Empress Dowager harshly: "After all she's only an ignorant woman, she never studied the classics." Father was very close to being treasonable himself.

There was no point now in Boon Jin's staying on at Geok Pin Academy. If government jobs were going to depend on being in favour with the authorities, rather than on good examination results, then he had already ruined his chances. Father let him know that he had let the family down; he was a disgrace, he didn't have the first filial virtue. "Wu zhun, wu fu!" Father said to him, "No respect for Emperor, no respect for parents!"

Boon Jin got this kind of recrimination throughout the months he stayed at home until after the Chinese New Year of 1906. He was glad to leave home, when the festival was over, to try to make a new start in Singapore.

# 3

Businessmen boast of their skill and cunning
But in philosophy they are like little children.

—*Chen Zu Ang, around 680 A.D.*

THE FIRST DAYS that Boon Jin spent in the rice warehouse were discouraging. Chua, the compradore, handed him a pile of accounts and asked him to work out the month's income and outgo. Boon Jin had learned nothing like this in school mathematics and he was baffled.

"I don't know how to do this," he said reluctantly.

"A young scholar like you cannot keep accounts? Then you had better sit quietly and read your book," Chua said kindly.

"I can help you to write letters," Boon Jin offered, but there was no correspondence at the warehouse.

The rice came to Singapore to be stored in the Tans' warehouse beside the river. It was sold again to small shopkeepers in the city, or to agents in the northern states. Uncle handled the correspondence from an office in town. At the warehouse Chua the compradore was in charge, and Uncle seldom came there.

Chua handled bills of lading and receipt, scrawled on scraps of yellow paper each with some merchant's vermilion chop. He kept the big ledgers, peering at them through his thick spectacles, rattling the beads of his abacus in a quick irregular rhythm which Boon Jin could not begin to equal.

Boon Jin asked his Uncle for a book on accounting, but Uncle scoffed.

"Where is there ever a classical text on business accounting? Some things cannot be studied from books. You must ask old Chua to teach you."

Old Chua could not, or would not, teach Boon Jin. "Never mind, I don't need your help," he said indulgently, like someone talking to a small child. "You just amuse yourself and do not bother about business matters."

For a while Boon Jin was content to occupy himself with getting to know his way around Singapore, and its society that was so strange to him.

As Boon Jin started to go about the city, he found that there were many other communities in Singapore, but they did not mix. The Indians and Malays and Europeans and Eurasians lived separate from each other. Even among the Chinese, Hokkiens did not mix with Cantonese, or Hylams with Teochews, or the English-educated Straits Chinese with the Chinese-educated.

He had noticed, on the first day he arrived, that the most

eminent Singapore Chinese in that big procession were merchants. There were no representatives of the scholars, gentlemen, nobles and court officials, who formed the upper classes in China. Boon Jin saw nobody in Singapore who seemed to belong to his own social world and he felt very isolated.

He often dreamed he was back home in China, catching crickets along the riverbank, or playing in the Happy Fragrance Garden among his mother's favourite flowers.

. . .

One morning he rode in the carriage with Uncle and Hock Joo to the Telok Ayer area, where Uncle had his office. Hock Joo, who expected to take over the business, showed off how well he knew his way around the office. There were two clerks writing in English, one dipping a steel-nibbed pen into ink and one clattering on a modern typewriter.

"I have a small job for you, Boon Jin," Uncle said. "I need to write a ceremonial sort of letter to Old Wong in Foochow, congratulating him on his sixtieth birthday. Let's see if you can write as nicely as the professional letter writer."

Boon Jin was glad he had kept practising his calligraphy, two hours every afternoon while Hock Joo stretched out and snored under the circling electric fan. He composed a few lines of elegant compliments and wrote them carefully in formal characters.

"What a time you took to write a simple letter," Uncle grumbled. "Well, look at these grand learned words! Old Wong won't understand half of it, he'll be really impressed!"

Somehow Boon Jin felt that, though Uncle was pleased with him, he didn't really appreciate his scholarship.

Near the office was what was obviously a school, with many boys in white uniforms moving around. Boon Jin, peering across, thought the teaching system rather strange. The students did not chant their lessons loudly as they did in China. The teacher, instead of sitting sternly at his desk, stood up writing on a board.

"That's Mr. Gan Eng Seng's Anglo-Chinese Free School," Hock Joo informed him. "They teach in Chinese and English, both. The Anglo-Chinese School that I go to is much better, we are taught only in English, by teachers from England," Hock Joo said with a superior air.

"If you do business in Amoy, you will need to be able to read and write Chinese," Boon Jin suggested gently.

"I shall do business in Singapore, not in Amoy. I shall trade with the British and Americans, in English. And if I need a letter to be written in Chinese, I shall hire some Chinese scholar like you to do it!"

Boon Jin still couldn't cope with this kind of blunt rudeness. Angry inside, he said a polite goodbye to Hock Joo and walked away.

He went down Telok Ayer Road, and passed a couple of big temples which had a familiar look; with red pillars and beams, green-tiled, up-turned roofs, carved dragons writhing among the incense fumes. As he got into Cross Street he saw fewer of the European horse carriages and fewer Indians and Malays. He was in Chinatown proper, "Water Bullock Cart Area". He was jostled by a rickshaw puller who swore in Amoy accents; he passed little stalls selling beancurd and seafood delicacies, he paused to inspect the calligraphy of the street-corner letter-writer. He began to feel more at home in Singapore.

It was still a foreign, highly Westernised country. In South Bridge Road there were electric trams running on steel rails. Boon Jin saw the tall pinnacle of an Indian temple whose gods and animal figures looked utterly bizarre to him. Then he walked round Smith Street and Sago Lane, and found that he had got into the unsavoury vice area, and re-emerged to South Bridge Road where he loitered, looking at the rows of small shops. There were goldsmiths, silversmiths, pawn shops, book shops, shops selling silks and Chinese medicines. He had changed some of his New Year gift money for Straits dollars; he bought a newspaper, and ate a bowl of soupy noodles at a stall.

The stallholders, used to dealing with all sorts of Chinese, showed no curiosity about Boon Jin. With his long hair down his back, wearing loose trousers and a jacket closed with cloth buttons down the front, he looked no different from other people on the street. He felt happy just to melt into the anonymous city crowd.

At last Boon Jin turned homeward. He passed the noisy rickshaw station at the foot of Neil Road—the sign saying "Jinrickshaw Station" may be there still—and so came back to Uncle's house; footsore, but feeling rather less lost and lonely.

. . .

Boon Jin smuggled his newspaper up to his room. Father might condemn newspapers as ephemeral trash, but there were no Chinese books in Uncle's house and Boon Jin was starved for something to read.

The newspaper was called *Nanyang Zong Hui Pao*, "*Union Times*", and its main pages were devoted to Chinese events; this seemed quite natural to Boon Jin who had not yet realised that anything important could happen outside China. He was fascinated to read a vigorous criticism of the Peking government, and a demand for the Parliamentary Constitution. Talk like this got people's heads chopped off in China.

The contributors to this newspaper were not afraid to sign their names—one of them, Boon Jin saw, was that eminent Dr. Lim Boon Keng. Another article in the same issue reported the visit to Singapore of a senior Chinese Minister—one known to be pro-Reform. The *Union Times* described him meeting the Chinese consul, shaking hands with the Governor, having dinner with local leaders including that same Dr. Lim. Boon Jin realised that, far from being cut off from China's political life, the Nanyang Chinese could contribute to it with greater freedom under the protecting umbrella of British colonialism. He wondered whether he could meet some of these people.

But he didn't breathe a word of this to Uncle, when Uncle said one evening that he ought to meet some of Singapore's important men. Uncle took him to the Chinese Chamber of Commerce in Hill Street and pointed out significant figures. "That is Lim the pineapple king, worth two million dollars; that one is Khoo Tiong Lay, his father planted rubber before anybody else and now he's the richest man in the country."

Boon Jin bowed politely to the big merchants but was not impressed. He just thought it was funny to honour men who did not belong to what he considered the upper classes. Uncle pointed out a certain great Mr. Gwee who wore the insignia of a Chinese Government official, a "Second Class Assistant Secretary in the Customs Department". He was another rich merchant who had simply bought the honorary title for money. Boon Jin thought this was even funnier.

Presently Boon Jin drifted away from his Uncle's side. He heard a Hokkien-speaking voice talking about China and went closer.

"China has wealth that other nations have always dreamed of. Now that China is opening up, there is going to be a tremendous competition for a share of it," the speaker was saying. His cheeks were plump and his stomach comfortably rounded out the front of his Western evening coat. He wore a carnation in his buttonhole. He had a black moustache, and a high square forehead and the hooded, searching eyes of a scholar.

"Experts of all kinds, translators and technicians, are needed in China today," he went on. "But what we need most are middlemen: people who understand both Western civilisation and Chinese. The Japanese are doing their best to do this, with the advantages of sharing Chinese writing and a lot of Chinese culture. But we Straits Chinese should be able to do it even better!"

It was Dr. Lim Boon Keng, saying in 1906 the kind of thing that might be heard in the Chinese Chamber of Commerce today, in its multi-storey building in Hill Street.

"The people in China tend to trust us more because we are Chinese like them. We can understand them better. At the same time we can communicate with Westerners and we're more used to Western pace and management styles. Why should we be missing all these opportunities? As Chinese, as sons of Han, why don't we too go out and get our share of the riches of China?"

There was a ripple of applause from the men standing around. Boon Jin was fascinated and listened hard.

"The important thing we must do," Dr. Lim went on, "is to learn to read and write the official language of China. Our children should learn Mandarin as well as English."

"We have discussed this before, Boon Keng," said someone. "A child's brain is only so big, it can't learn two languages at once, as well as other lessons."

"It depends on the desire to learn," Lim Boon Keng said. "A good student can manage it." He was looking straight at Boon Jin, who had been trying to hide himself behind the older men.

"And you want to teach literature in the schools, Boon Keng," the other person continued. "Now that's absurd. Shakespeare or the Chinese Classics, we don't need them!"

"Our people in the Nanyang are so starved of true education that they don't even know what they are missing. Didn't Lu Xiang Shan say: 'Study of the Classics aids morality…' I forget, how does the quotation go?"

He looked at Boon Jin again, with an encouraging smile; putting no pressure in it however, and Boon Jin could simply have looked away if he hadn't known the answer. He did know it. He recited shyly: "Moral principles are inherent in the mind, endowed by Heaven but beclouded by material desires. Study of the Confucian Classics develops this inborn ethical sense."

"Thank you! Yes, the Classics are the foundation of Chinese

virtues. But in Singapore neither the immigrant peasants, nor the English-educated Babas, know anything about our own ancient culture. They are like plants without roots: they have no base to develop good moral principles and character. That is why I am so devoted to spreading the knowledge of the Confucian classics. I hope you gentlemen will continue to give your financial support to our schools."

The group broke up. Dr. Lim Boon Keng beckoned to Boon Jin who was diffidently hanging about.

"That was a good answer, young man. You have studied the Confucian Classics, haven't you?"

"How did you know, sir?"

"A doctor learns to look at people," said Dr. Lim, carefully lighting a cigar. "Education shapes character, character is shown in the face. Is your family a scholarly one?"

Dr. Lim was a very important man in Singapore, and old enough to be Boon Jin's father, but he was very easy to talk to. Boon Jin found himself telling all about his family; he didn't realise how late it was till Uncle came and interrupted them, not looking at all pleased.

"Boon Jin! Why are you pestering Dr. Lim? Dr. Lim, I am sorry my nephew is making a nuisance of himself."

"I'm very pleased to have met your nephew," Dr. Lim told Uncle reassuringly. "Boon Jin: I was telling you that we run regular classes to teach the Mandarin language to our children.

Your good father has taught you a very pure Mandarin accent. I wonder whether you could help with our classes?"

Boon Jin would have liked nothing better, but with Uncle standing beside he had to refuse. "I'm sorry, I am already working for my Uncle."

"Never mind. Come and join in our discussion group sometimes. Our Good Learning Society, Hao-Shueh Hui, meets every Thursday night."

Boon Jin stammered some sort of thanks as Uncle dragged him away.

. . .

"Stay away from Dr. Lim Boon Keng. He's a trouble-maker," scolded Uncle.

"A trouble-maker!" Boon Jin repeated in surprise. "I thought he was someone in authority—he meets the Chinese consul and the English governor."

"Authority, Lim Boon Keng has no authority," Uncle snorted. "Because he went to Europe to study medicine, and can speak English well, he got a seat on the Legislative Council, and they call on him to chair public meetings and make speeches. But he has no money of his own, no family, no real weight. He is just a politician."

Why would an ordinary citizen want to concern himself

with public affairs, Uncle asked. No one who wasn't born into the ruling classes would bother, unless he had something to gain from it. Lim Boon Keng must be greedy and opportunistic. If there was no evidence that he was corrupt, that just showed he was crafty too.

Furthermore, "it's well-known that he is in league with recognised traitors against the Emperor. When the notorious Kang Yu Wei fled from Imperial wrath, Lim Boon Keng helped to hide him in Singapore. All the newspapers had the story."

Boon Jin was most interested, but Uncle would not tell him any more and he did not get the full story till some time later. Then he heard how in 1900 Dr. Lim invited Kang Yu Wei to come to Singapore. Kang stayed hidden at a friend's house for a while, till rumours spread that the Empress Dowager's agents had arrived in Singapore to find him.

The British Governor didn't want Kang murdered in his territory—British honour was involved. He sent for Dr. Lim Boon Keng, that reliable Chinaman who spoke English as well as he did himself.

Dr. Lim let it be known that Kang Yu Wei was leaving Singapore. Anyone interested saw Kang going up the gangplank of the P & O liner and sailing away. Almost no one saw him coming back, half an hour later, in a British government launch. He stayed in Singapore another month, at another safe house, preaching Reform and organising his Restore the Emperor Society.

Local newspaper reporters eventually found out the details and splashed the scoop all over the front pages. The Peking Government, too weak for a direct protest to London, issued a harsh warning to Lim Boon Keng. Peking threatened the lives of Dr. Lim as a rebel, and of any relatives he had in China. If he wanted to be a patriot he should serve the Chinese Government.

Since then, Dr. Lim had apparently thoroughly rehabilitated himself, as far as the Chinese Government was concerned. He was on the best of terms with the Chinese consul and any visiting officials. He had been invited to Peking by the Minister for the Interior and offered an official post. All the same, people like Uncle remembered he had been in trouble, and distrusted him.

If Boon Jin visited Dr. Lim, said Uncle, it would be reported in China by the Government agents. It could have serious consequences for his family at home, did Boon Jin want that to happen, was he so unfilial and undutiful?

Having said this, it never occurred to Uncle that Boon Jin might disobey. He never knew that Boon Jin was sneaking away to the meetings of Lim Boon Keng's Good Learning Society, half disbelieving Uncle's warnings, in any case wholly unable to stay away.

Dr. Lim Boon Keng was like no one Boon Jin had ever met before. He was a Singapore-born Chinese with a worldwide breadth of vision. He quoted Confucius and the Classics, but had been unable to read any Chinese till after leaving Edinburgh University. He was highly cultured and educated, but he had been labelled a rebel for talking Reform.

He seemed to spend all his time minding other people's business. As a medical man, he crusaded against drug abuse through the Anti-Opium Society, and against the binding of women's feet. As a Chinese patriot he contributed to the *Union Times*, as a Singaporean to the *Straits Chinese Magazine*. He had represented his people on the Legislative Council. As an educationist he founded schools, and supported the Hao-Shueh Society. Perhaps he was responsible for that society's high-sounding English name, an erudite derivation from two Greek words—the Philomathic Society.

"A Chinese patriot is one who wants the best for China," Boon Jin heard Dr. Lim saying, the first evening that he went to the Philomathic Society. "A wise emperor, supported by a democratic form of government; modern reorganisation to bring back national prosperity, and social reforms to help the starving peasants. Mr. Kang Yu Wei's Restore the Emperor Society, to which I am proud to belong, is truly patriotic."

Boon Jin absorbed this attentively. He remembered how his father had called him "Wu zhun, wu fu!"—no loyalty to

Emperor, no filial piety—someone without one elementary virtue. That night Boon Jin lay awake and imagined that he was talking to his father; explaining to Father that you could want reform for China, without being disloyal to the Emperor.

The serious, high-minded thinkers of the Philomathic Society often reproached the wealthy Babas of Singapore for frittering away their time and money on gambling, partying and generally amusing themselves. They were proud that there was one rich Baba in the Philomathic Society: the wealthiest of them all, the rubber magnate Khoo Tiong Lay.

It was Khoo Tiong Lay who told Boon Jin the story of how Dr. Lim Boon Keng had helped Kang Yu Wei escape from the Chinese Government agents. Khoo sat down beside Boon Jin one evening, when the other members of the Philomathic Society were discussing literary matters, and asked him if he knew about Reform activities in the past. Boon Jin was most impressed to hear of the close link between Dr. Lim and the great Reformer.

"I understand that Mr. Kang lives in Penang now," he said to Mr. Khoo, at the same time wondering why the millionaire was bothering with a young student like himself. "Does Dr. Lim still correspond with him?"

"You admire Mr. Kang very much, don't you?" remarked Khoo Tiong Lay. Like other rich Babas, Khoo had been educated in English. Since he'd come to know Lim Boon Keng, he had learned some Mandarin. In his conversation and dress and manners, he was like an English gentleman; but beneath his smooth geniality, there was the arrogance of a man to whom people had, throughout his life, been very, very polite. "But has it occurred to you, Tan Boon Jin, that with all his fine ideas Kang Yu Wei has not been able to achieve anything for the good of China?"

"He was not allowed to," protested Boon Jin. "He and the enlightened Emperor tried to carry out great reforms, but they were prevented."

"Exactly so! The fact is that the Manchus who rule China, the great Ministers and Court advisers, will never allow any progress. China's only hope of salvation is to overthrow the Qing government, and drive the Manchus out of China!"

Boon Jin stared at Khoo Tiong Lay with startled eyes. He had heard revolutionary talk before, from madmen like Teochew Hoon. He had not expected to hear such talk in the Philomathic Society, from the richest man in Singapore.

"Have you heard of Dr. Sun Yat Sen?" Khoo Tiong Lay continued, dropping his voice slightly. "Perhaps you didn't know that Dr. Lim helped Dr. Sun out of trouble too, around the same time as the Kang Yu Wei incident. Two of Dr. Sun's Japanese friends were arrested in Singapore. Dr. Lim spoke to the British Governor and got them out of jail."

Even with this recommendation, Boon Jin had heard only

bad about Sun Yat Sen. He said hesitantly: "I was told that Dr. Sun organised a big rebellion in Canton, and helped the peasants get swords and rifles to fight against the government soldiers."

"You are right. Again and again in the past ten years, Dr. Sun has organised the people of the Southern provinces to rebel against the Manchu overlords. Each time the government has crushed the rebels without mercy, but we have never given up hope. Even today, we are collecting money to finance yet another attempt to cast off the Manchu yoke! One battle may be lost, but the struggle for freedom will continue!"

Khoo had spoken louder in his enthusiasm and Dr. Lim turned round from his conversation nearby.

"What's that, Tiong Lay? Are you preaching revolution to our young friend? That won't do, or you'll have him going off to join Sun Yat Sen, to death and dishonour!" Dr. Lim laughed and made a joke of it all. "His good uncle won't thank you for that!"

"No, I won't go to join the rebels," Boon Jin promised, laughing shyly.

"I am telling him that I don't think the Manchus will ever allow China to change," said Khoo Tiong Lay.

"That is demonstrably untrue," Dr. Lim said sharply. "You are simply ignoring the steps China has already taken towards democracy. The Empress Dowager has actually set up a special

Bureau to prepare a political constitution for China, and it was peaceful, non-violent public pressure that persuaded her to do so. We Overseas Chinese helped to exert that pressure—you yourself, Tiong Lay, put your signature on the petition we sent to Peking!"

"Well, we shall see whether that Bureau produces any result," shrugged Khoo.

"Meanwhile, let's have no more talk about violent revolution," Dr. Lim said; and he moved across to talk to Boon Jin, as though to protect him from Khoo.

"I'm glad you have been coming to our meetings, Tan Boon Jin. What did you think of Mr. Song Ong Siang's talk on Macbeth?"

"I am afraid I don't understand English," Boon Jin replied.

"You should learn! I could help you a little," Dr. Lim offered. "If you come round to my clinic in Telok Ayer Street, I am quite unoccupied during tiffin time every day."

• • •

Next day, during his lunch hour, Dr. Lim began teaching Boon Jin to read and write English.

The letters of the alphabet were already quite familiar to Boon Jin, from English posters and advertisements. Now he was fascinated by the way that each letter had its own sound and the sounds could be fitted together. He could recognise the shape of a few English words which he had often seen, and he tried to pronounce them according to their spelling: "Raleigh Bicycle".

"Unfortunately English spelling is not consistent," Dr. Lim explained. "Human beings are not completely rational, which is the cause of much tragedy! Some words just have to be memorised: you will not find that difficult."

Another interesting thing was that the alphabet wasn't confined to the English language. "The Romans wrote Latin with this alphabet. It can be used to write English, or Malay, or even romanised vernacular Hokkien," said Dr. Lim, demonstrating them all; though he believed—and Boon Jin heartily agreed with him—that classical Chinese must always be written in its beautiful characters, which could never be replaced by the Roman alphabet.

So when he had mastered the alphabet, Boon Jin thought it only natural to start learning to use it to read Malay as well as English. Dr. Lim gave him every encouragement, neither of them thinking that Boon Jin might be tackling too much. After all, Dr. Lim had learned classical Chinese and Malay, by private study in his spare time.

Boon Jin saw why Lim Boon Keng, still relatively young, with no other asset but education, had already become the foremost public figure among the Straits Chinese.

"I have never grown tired of learning," Confucius said, "nor wearied in teaching others what I have learned." Dr. Lim Boon Keng could have said the same.

# 4

> Fifty-sixth hexagram: the first line,
> Divided, shows the stranger in lowly position,
> Unworthily occupied.
> It is thus that he brings on himself calamity.
>
> —*The I Ching*

Boon Jin had been more than half a year in Singapore, and still felt out of place in Uncle's household. He thought that he would not feel at home with that family, if he stayed with them for the rest of his life. It wasn't because they lacked classical education. It was because they were so narrow-minded and complacent. They thought that the money they owned, and the things they bought with it, were more important than anything else in the world.

Boon Jin was too insecure himself, to reflect that they could not help being ignorant. He wondered whether his Father knew that he was sending Boon Jin to live with people who rejected the values of his home. Either Father hadn't bothered to find out, or he knew and didn't care: either way, Boon Jin felt he had just been thrown away, the way that poor peasants sometimes left a baby girl out to die.

He had been sent to the Nanyang to make his fortune, but his vague hopes of becoming Uncle's indispensable right-hand man, a budding business tycoon, had faded. Every morning he went to the rice warehouse but old Chua still had no work for him to do. The only thing he could do was read, six hours a day, as he had been used to studying all his life. No one disturbed him. He sat at a little desk among the cool dusty sacks of rice, and read the books Dr. Lim lent him.

"Tan Boon Jin, you should read Darwin's *On the Origin of Species*," Dr. Lim might begin, and his cigar would be left to smoulder unheeded in its tray while his eyes lit up with enthusiasm. "His theory is that the human race was evolved through a process of natural selection, from the lower animals! I can't find a translation into Chinese; can you read the English?" Boon Jin thought he could understand about half the words. "That's splendid, take this dictionary and you'll manage. Here are some little Malay tales you might enjoy. And to relax with, here's a translation into classical Chinese, of Dickens' *A Tale of Two Cities*: some people think Liang Chi Chao's version is better than the original!"

When he returned the books, Dr. Lim would discuss them with him. "What do you think of Darwin's theory? Many people condemn it simply because it seems to contradict the

Christian Scriptures. But quoting classical writings won't answer scientific questions! You must assess the evidence, and weigh arguments on both sides."

Boon Jin began to keep a journal on what he was reading. Today the old cloth-bound notebook can be seen in the archives of Wenguang Academy. The pages, filled with Boon Jin's beautiful grass-style characters, record his mental adventures during those months of 1906.

He already had a sound basic education in the Chinese classics. Had he continued with his formal education, he would have gone on refining his literary style and deepening his knowledge of ancient writers. He would have been closely supervised by tutors and kept within well-trodden paths of thought. Instead, he started exploring the exciting wide world of Western science and literature; mostly on his own, with some guidance from Dr. Lim. In later years, Boon Jin became an influential writer and essayist within the international Chinese community. His growth as an independent thinker began during this rather depressed period of his life in Singapore.

• • •

When he had studied enough for the day, Boon Jin would ramble around Singapore town, walking for hours through the crowded streets. One evening he fell into bad company.

He was roaming through Water Bullock Cart district after dark had fallen: the streets, lit by glaring electric lamps, were as bustling as during the day. Near the Cantonese Opera House he passed the clinic of a traditional Chinese physician. A card on the door said: "A lecture on the Classics will be given at One Leaf House this evening." On impulse, Boon Jin thought he would go in and meet the Confucian students.

Several people were already waiting for the lecture to begin, in a room at the back of the clinic. They did not look much like the students of Geok Pin Academy. They seemed to be tradesmen, and shop assistants, and a few might even have been gangsters. Boon Jin thought that trying to teach the Classics to such people would be a waste of time.

The physician, Mr. Yu Lieh, came in. He spoke in Cantonese, which Boon Jin could follow with some difficulty. He began by announcing the text on which he would lecture.

"Mencius says: 'The people are the most important element in the nation; the spirits of the grain and land are next; the Prince is the last.'"

Beginning with this text, the lecturer spoke of the rights of the people, and the ruler's duty to take unselfish care of his people, or else lose his position. From this he went on to condemn the Qing government and to call for revolution. Boon Jin realised he had got into a clandestine indoctrination cell, handing out propaganda under the guise of education. He began to wish he had not come.

The physician referred to the revolutionary leader, Dr. Sun Yat Sen. He spoke of some great international society this man had founded, dedicated to overthrowing the Qing government. Apparently the physician of One Leaf House was looking for recruits!

This was really dangerous talk. Boon Jin became very apprehensive. After the lecture he tried to slip out quietly but a tough-looking man stopped him. "Who are you? What are you doing here?"

"I'm not doing any harm...I just came in to hear the teacher." For the first time in his life, Boon Jin pretended to be dumber than he was. "I couldn't understand what he said. I want to learn about Confucius."

"What is your name? Are you a spy?"

"I know this young man. I'll recommend him," said a voice. It was Khoo Tiong Lay, looking rather incongruous there in his well-tailored Western suit.

"What are you doing in this part of town, Tan Boon Jin?"

"I came in to hear a lecture on the Classics," Boon Jin repeated stubbornly.

"Yes, I remember you're a Classical student," said Khoo Tiong Lay. "Well, you had better get home quickly. You won't speak of what you've heard here, will you?"

"No never," Boon Jin promised, knowing that there was a threat behind the genial slap on the shoulder that Khoo gave him.

"Wait a moment," Khoo said. "I have a little book here that I would like to give you. Read it when you have time, and tell me what you think of it!"

He put a small booklet into Boon Jin's hands. Boon Jin thanked him and hurried off, very glad to have come to no harm.

. . .

At his desk in the warehouse next day, Boon Jin examined the pamphlet that Khoo Tiong Lay had given him. It was called *The Revolutionary Army*. He had heard it praised, but never seen a copy. He settled down to read it carefully.

As he read the opening paragraphs his eyes widened in delight. They were written in clear modern language—the language of common everyday speech, not of literary classics; Boon Jin whistled under his breath in admiration. He read on, and started frowning. In his colloquial, dramatic style, the author was launching a diatribe of racialist hatred against the Manchu rulers of China.

He talked about past Manchu atrocities against Han Chinese, and about present discriminations. He said that the

Manchus were responsible for all of China's problems; he said they were systematically oppressing the Chinese on racial lines, and doing their best to destroy them as a people.

"All Chinese must rise to wage a bloody war against the Manchus, to destroy their power and drive them out of China!"

The language was very strong. The ideas it presented were also clear and simple: an ardent call to Han nationalism, a single-minded cry for revenge, a clear solution for all of China's problems. No wonder that this pamphlet had been banned in China, while being immensely popular among revolutionary students.

But Boon Jin, with his family traditions of Imperial service, couldn't suddenly start regarding the Emperor of China as an alien. Trying to be objective, he remembered that other dynasties had begun as conquering barbarians, who were now regarded as part of China's heritage. He remembered that the Qing Emperor Chien Lung, under whom his great-grandfather had served, had been an enlightened Confucian ruler, surely no enemy of the Chinese people.

He wondered what to say, when he returned the pamphlet to Khoo Tiong Lay at the next meeting of the Philomathic Society. He could be polite and honest, in saying that he much admired the literary style. If pressed, he would have to say that he rejected the racialist theme.

But the occasion for saying this never arose. Boon Jin never went to another meeting of the Philomathic Society.

• • •

Uncle never seemed to ask what Boon Jin was doing. Studying so hard, he did not think he was wasting his time. All the same, Boon Jin kept wishing that he could do something to impress Uncle and make himself seem more useful. One day, as he watched the daily work of the warehouse, he noticed something which he thought he should tell his uncle.

Rice was being brought into the warehouse from a junk which had just come from China. The ship was moored at the river wharf and a plank stretched from its deck to the quay in front of the warehouse. A labourer ran down the plank, carrying a sack of rice on his shoulder. He trotted through the door of the warehouse and flung his sack down in the shadows. He loped out again into the blazing sunlight and joined the line of labourers unloading the ship.

The bags of rice were stacked high in the hold. The head of the labour-gang stood on the pile. As each labourer lined up below him, he heaved up a heavy sack and swung it to the labourer's shoulder.

He handled the sacks with a heavy iron hook, which he thrust into each bag through the coarse material. Then he pulled out the hook, with a jerk and a twist: more of a jerk than necessary, Boon Jin thought as he observed, and the cloth tore a little. A thin stream of rice grains fell, as the labourer jogged across the wharf into the warehouse.

A child darted from somewhere and scampered among the men's feet, with a brush and pan. He swept up the spilled rice and disappeared. No one heeded him; he gleaned the fallen grains, like the fat pigeons that pecked in the dust of the quays.

Chua stood watching the unloading. He saw Boon Jin looking at the skittering child. "The poor must do what they can to survive," he smiled. "Tan's company is rich enough to give help to the poor."

A friend of Chua's was with him: a tall, muscular fellow with a green dragon tattooed on his left arm, who seemed to spend all his time lounging about the wharves and godowns. "It is charity, little scholar, only charity," he said, and he and Chua laughed together.

Even Boon Jin, whose life had been relatively sheltered, knew that the tattoo was a mark of secret society membership, and that it would be better not to offend the man who wore it. So he pretended not to mind being made fun of; but the incident made him keep his eyes open. A few days later he noticed the gangster loafing near the godown, with a sack near his feet. The ragged child skulked up to him and handed over a cloth bag, rounded with the weight of whatever it held. The contents of the bag went into the sack.

That evening Boon Jin tried to tell his Uncle about this. "Uncle, this is organised stealing. A few pounds of rice from every ship unloaded on the wharves, could amount to a sack of rice every day. The gangsters can sell it for profit, at our expense."

But Uncle brushed him aside. "A few grains of rice here and there, what do they matter!"

"It is still stealing anyway. And old Chua must know all about it," Boon Jin persisted.

"Never mind, it's not important!" Uncle said angrily. "Don't stir things up and make trouble."

Much later, Boon Jin understood that Uncle was fully aware of the secret society rackets, but was afraid to do anything about them. His long-term plan was that Boon Jin should eventually take over Chua's work, although he had never properly considered how Boon Jin was to learn the job. Meanwhile, Uncle just let Chua do as he liked. For he knew, as Boon Jin had not realised, that Chua was a powerful officer in the secret society.

Boon Jin kept observing the movements of rice in and out of the warehouse. He thought that there might be other, more significant, ways in which rice was being stolen. Could the sacks of rice be under weight, for example? When buyers' carts came to carry sacks of rice away, did Chua keep correct count of the bags of rice taken out of the warehouse? He just stood joking and chatting with the agents while labourers loaded the bullock carts. He could be writing fictitious figures into the ledgers, and saying that any shortages were due to damage done by rats in the warehouse.

Boon Jin pondered how he could check his suspicions. He imagined himself finding proof of Chua's dishonesty, and bringing him to justice like a famous judge in old stories. Uncle would be immensely pleased and grateful, and write to Father with many praises for him.

The next time a bullock cart was being loaded with sacks of rice, it wasn't so difficult for Boon Jin to count the sacks that left the warehouse. He did it discreetly, pretending to be reading his book. He watched Chua making the entry in his ledger.

The ledger was kept in Chua's big desk, together with a cash box, and because of the cash box the desk was kept locked whenever Chua was away. That evening Boon Jin stayed back reading, when Chua locked his desk as usual, and put on his white solar topee to go home.

. . .

"Still working so hard, little scholar?" Chua mocked as he passed Boon Jin. He went away and Boon Jin was alone in the shadowy warehouse.

He got out a little black-handled English screwdriver that he had bought in South Bridge Road. The drawer was closed by a padlock in a staple. Very carefully Boon Jin took out the screws. The staple came loose and the drawer opened; the big ledger was inside, next to the blue cash box. Boon Jin took the ledger back to his own desk to examine it.

He turned to the last entries in the book and looked at what Chua had written for that day. "Twenty-three bags for Chop Wee Shing," Chua had written. Boon Jin had counted twenty-five bags of rice being loaded. The other entries were wrong too: always fewer bags recorded than Boon Jin had counted being sent away. He had proof of Chua's dishonesty.

He put the ledger back and replaced the screws. The old Indian watchman came shuffling through the shadows to his charpoy bed among the rice bags. "Are you working late, Master?" he said in Malay.

"I had a lot to study," Boon Jin answered, picking up his books. He walked home. He was late for dinner and his Uncle wanted to know where he had been.

"I was just walking around town," Boon Jin said.

"Another time, come straight home," said Uncle. "What would your father say, if he knew that you spend your free time wandering about the streets like a loafer?"

His cousin made a snide comment. Boon Jin sat quietly

through the dinner, thinking that soon he would be able to surprise Uncle.

Next morning Boon Jin sat as usual at his desk. Bullock carts drove up to the warehouse to be loaded; the ragged child darted about with his brush and pan. Chua sat behind his desk, joking with the supervisors who came in to talk to him. Boon Jin counted every bag of rice that was taken out of the warehouse. He had compiled a long list, before he went out at noonday for his meal.

When Boon Jin returned to the warehouse he was surprised to find Uncle there, talking to Chua. "Where have you been?" Uncle asked angrily. "Mr. Chua has been telling me bad news about you: you are lazy and idle, you are a nuisance to him."

Chua was smiling mildly, apologetically. "What I said is, there is nothing here for a scholar to do. This is not the right place for him."

"What do you do here every day, all day? Are you wasting your time?"

"No, Uncle, I'm not wasting my time. May I speak to you privately?"

"Privately? What for?"

"I will tell you something important, which no one else should hear."

Grumbling, Uncle moved with Boon Jin a few steps out of the warehouse onto the quay. Boon Jin told Uncle his suspicions.

"Uncle, they are stealing rice from you every day. I have looked at the books and I am sure of what I am saying. Today I counted the bags of rice taken away. All you have to do is to look at the figures Chua wrote down."

"You're sure? You're very sure?" Uncle asked, frowning.

"I'm willing to die, if this isn't true," Boon Jin said.

Uncle went back to Chua. Instead of accusing him, he spoke in tactful terms. "My nephew has been trying his skill by making a record of the bags of rice taken from the warehouse. He has asked me to check his ability by comparing his list against your record."

"Of course, of course, here is my record of today's consignments," Chua said. He gave Uncle the big ledger, opened at the page for that day.

"Let us compare with the young master's record then," said Chua, beaming as always. "The first consignment today was to Chop Eng Kee: eighteen bags. You have eighteen written there? Good, good. Next we have twelve bags to Chop Soon Huat; then fifteen, nineteen, twenty, eighteen. Ah, here the young scholar has counted twenty-three, but really you see that we sold twenty-four: never mind, he is not experienced!"

Chua's records for that day showed no sign of dishonesty. Boon Jin gazed at Uncle's furious face, not knowing what to say.

"I do not like to speak badly about your nephew," said Chua.

"I have to tell you that last night, my night watchman says, the young man was creeping about the warehouse in the dusk, behaving very suspiciously. This morning, I found money missing from my desk."

"I didn't steal!" Boon Jin exclaimed.

"Look at this, sir." Chua brought out the blue enamel cash box: it had been forced open, and it was empty.

"I didn't touch it!"

"Mr. Tan, I think perhaps you should look through your nephew's belongings," Chua said. Uncle stalked over to Boon Jin's desk and searched it. Among the books he found the little black-handled screwdriver.

"What does a scholar, a young gentleman, want with a tool like that?" said Chua, looking on. "My drawer was stealthily opened, the screws taken out with a screwdriver: you can see marks if you look carefully. The cash box was forced open with some instrument."

"I never touched that cash box!" Boon Jin said loudly. "I opened the drawer to look at the books, to prove your dishonesty. I am not a thief. I would never steal money."

"Hah!" Uncle had hauled all the books out of the desk. He pulled out a piece of cloth wrapped round something heavy. He shook it. Six silver dollars fell out clinking, and rolled on the floor.

Boon Jin stared unbelievingly at the money. "Someone put

it there!" he gasped.

"You damned devil!" Uncle shouted at Boon Jin. "You cursed thief, you ungrateful monster. When your family hears about this your mother will hang herself for shame. Your father will strike your name out of the family records. You useless son, you make your family's name black. A child like you is better dead."

Uncle's voice was very loud. The nearby labourers stopped their work. People looked in through the door of the warehouse. Curious, staring eyes surrounded them. Uncle ignored them and went on shouting for a long time.

Boon Jin stood without moving, hanging his head. This was far worse than when Father had beaten him. Bruises could be healed. Boon Jin would never forget this public humiliation, beside the sunny river, with Chua smiling to himself nearby and onlookers gaping on every side.

Chua had set a trap and Boon Jin had fallen into it. He had not proved his case, and Uncle, afraid of the secret societies, had to disassociate himself from Boon Jin's suspicions. "Good for nothing, worthless, useless! Thief, rascal! Well, you have wasted enough time here. Apologise to Mr. Chua for breaking his desk, and come home with me."

Boon Jin looked at Chua, this man who had brought him into disgrace; he thought it would kill him to apologise to Chua. He turned and ran away from the warehouse.

"Boon Jin, come back!" Uncle shouted. Boon Jin disobeyed

and kept on running, up along the river side towards town.

* * *

He hurried through the streets hardly looking at the people and traffic around him. If the electric tram knocked him down, he thought bitterly, that would solve all his problems! Angry and miserable, he wanted to do something violent; he kept thinking of famous people who committed suicide to protest against some form of injustice.

He came out of his gloomy thoughts when there was a disturbance ahead of him in Cross Street. Loud voices were shouting: "Fight! Fight! Teochew comrades, come and fight!"

All the street people who didn't want to get involved in secret society fighting got out of the way fast. Hawkers picked up their baskets and ran; stallholders pushed their carts clattering over the stones. In moments Boon Jin was standing alone in a deserted street: and he could see the samsengs, armed with knives and iron bars, coming down the street. He ran.

The secret societies were fighting over their waterfront protection rackets. The fighting would spread across town, from Tanjong Pagar up into Serangoon. The Chinese consul and Dr. Lim Boon Keng and other Chinese leaders went round trying to talk peace to the combatants, but it was four days before the town was calm again.

Boon Jin didn't know all this. His moodiness had evaporated when he ran into real danger. Hurrying down Wayang Street he wanted to turn up South Bridge Road to go back to Uncle's house, but the shouting and fighting seemed to be worse in that direction. He decided to go back to the rice warehouse for safety. He could stay there all night if necessary.

He ran down Havelock Road. As he got near the warehouse he slowed down, panting for breath. The riverside lanes seemed to be deserted. Then a small group of men came towards him, holding heavy sticks. Boon Jin recognised the man with the green dragon tattoo. They were not just rioters: they were coming for him.

Boon Jin turned to run but in twenty steps they had grabbed him. He struggled but it was quite useless. "We'll teach you not to interfere with us, little scholar!"

The gangsters beat him with their heavy sticks. One blow across his ribs knocked him down; another blow made him think his legs were broken. The next blow struck his head. He was unconscious, when the gangsters picked up his limp body and dumped him into the Singapore River.

# 5

> Where there is true friendship,
> even water tastes sweet.
>
> —*Chinese proverb*

Waking was like being reborn, on the far side of a tremendous gulf. Boon Jin was coughing up water and someone was hurting him by pressing his chest. He felt sick and aching all over. He passed out again. He woke another time and found himself lying in the bottom of a small boat, too weak to move. Someone his own age leaned over him, saying something encouraging. An older man rowed the boat; behind him the sky was blue and brilliant.

The boat came to a white sandy beach. Boon Jin was helped ashore to a small hut under the coconut palms. He was shown a simple bed under a mosquito net, and he slept for a long time.

• • •

When he woke up the room was getting dark and a girl

brought an oil lamp into the room. "Ah, you're awake!" she said cheerfully, pulling back the mosquito net.

The boy from the boat was with her. "How do you feel?" he said. They spoke in Teochew-Hokkien. Boon Jin had had a Teochew nursemaid when he was very small. Automatically he answered in the simple language of childhood.

"I'm all right now. Thank you for looking after me!"

"I'm glad you're feeling better," the girl said. "You had a great bang on the head. You're bruised all over, too, my father said you might have a broken rib, but he's bandaged you up. How did you fall into the sea?"

"Don't bother him, Quek Choo," the youth said. "My sister will kill you with her chatter."

"Was I in the sea?" Boon Jin said wonderingly. He didn't know how he could have got there.

"Come and eat something," said the girl. She carried the oil lamp while her brother, Chong Beng, helped Boon Jin to get up and hobble to the outer room. At the eating table sat a man with a shrunken, crippled leg, who made Boon Jin welcome with a few words. He was Lim Chew, the father of Quek Choo and Chong Beng. He was a fish dealer. He and Chong Beng had been sailing their boat past the mouth of the Singapore River, when they found Boon Jin in the water.

"Some men attacked me and beat me at the riverside," Boon Jin told them.

"Probably they threw you into the river," said Lim Chew. "Were they robbers, or gangsters? There was rioting all over town, a lot of people were killed. Well, we must get you back to your family, mustn't we? They will be worrying about you."

Boon Jin hesitated. "Mr. Lim, I don't want to go back to my people right now. I'm in trouble at home. Someone convinced the uncle whom I'm staying with that I stole some money."

"How could anyone do that?" Quek Choo exclaimed. Boon Jin related how he had suspected Chua, and Chua had set a trap for him.

"So my uncle believes I stole the money. I can't do anything to prove that I'm innocent! But I tell you on my honour, I didn't steal!"

"Yes, I believe you! If you had really stolen money, you would not have told us a word about it," Chong Beng said, and his father nodded in agreement.

"I think you are honest, Tan Boon Jin," Lim Chew said. "So, if you don't want me to take you back to your Uncle's house, what are you going to do?"

"Please let me stay with you for a few days. I will be most grateful for your tolerance and generosity," Boon Jin said, using literary phrases without meaning to do so.

"You might as well stay till your bruises are better," Lim Chew consented.

"I shall have to depend on your hospitality," Boon Jin added diffidently. He could see from the bare wooden hut that the fish dealer was quite poor. "I don't have any money."

"Never mind!' Chong Beng and his father said together. "Don't talk about money!"

"A thin boy like you won't eat much rice!" Quek Choo said cheerfully. Boon Jin was very touched by their simple generosity.

• • •

When Boon Jin woke next morning, Lim Chew and his son had gone out on their daily work. Boon Jin got up carefully—his bruises were still very painful—and limped to the front of the house.

Lim Chew's small wooden house stood a little way from the group of Malay houses raised on stilts, which formed the fishing kampong of Siglap. It resembled the village dwellings of China, with the door set in the middle; in front a row of wooden posts held up the attap roof, and enclosed a verandah where people might sit in the evenings.

The house stood on a white beach at the edge of the sea, surrounded by thin grass and coconut trees. Where the grass ended there were heaps of loose dry sand, blinding white under the sun; below this sloped the beach packed smooth by the tide, without a single footprint on it. The sea was calm and clear. Tiny warm waves touched the sand as gently as ripples in a cup of tea.

Quek Choo was hanging clothes on a washing line between two trees. "Don't walk around too much, Boon Jin," she said. "You should rest and heal faster."

"I'd like to stay out here for a while."

"I'll get you a mat and you can lie under the trees." Quek Choo helped Boon Jin to stretch out on a grass mat in the shade of a broad-leaved tree. He lay there all morning watching Quek Choo go in and out. When her housework was done she fed her chickens and watered her vegetable garden; she never seemed to sit still.

"Aren't you hot? Don't you want to come inside?" she said at noonday.

"Really, I'm very happy here," Boon Jin said.

"As long as you're happy!" Quek Choo laughed, grinning all over her thin, dark face. "I'll bring your rice outside and we can eat under the trees!"

"Like Po Chu-I drinking under the trees," Boon Jin said, forgetting to keep his literary quotations to himself. But Quek Choo didn't laugh at him. She brought out a meal and squatted on the grass to eat with him. She hauled Boon Jin's mat around to the cool side of the tree and went on with her work, coming to chat with Boon Jin from time to time through the long afternoon.

Today the beach where Lim Chew's house stood lies a full mile away from the sea, under a busy road. It was quite lonely in Boon Jin's time. No one walked along the sand. The sea stretched to a horizon of hazy blue land. A boat or two from the nearby village rowed across the sparkling sea. The coconut fronds rustled above Boon Jin's head. All afternoon he watched the tide creeping down the beach, exposing the mudflats where crabs scampered, and the long sand bank further out. It was the most quiet and peaceful day he could remember.

• • •

During that day Boon Jin thought hard about his future. He felt that he could not bear to return to Uncle's house. Slowly he began to think that he did not have to go back.

The men who had attacked him were Chua's secret society men. Boon Jin guessed that Chua wanted to get rid of him for interfering, and had taken the chance of the riots to have him murdered in the confusion. They had dropped him into the river. They thought he was dead. If he never went back to the house, Uncle would assume that he had been killed somewhere in the riots.

Boon Jin didn't feel easy in deciding to let his family think he was dead. But he could see a chance for a new kind of life in front of him. He would make his fortune, and one day he would go home and surprise everyone. His parents would be overjoyed to find that he wasn't dead after all; he would bow to them, and give them money that would solve all their problems.

So Boon Jin daydreamed, to soothe his guilty feelings, and he made up his mind that he wouldn't go back.

He said this to Lim Chew that evening, when Chong Beng and his father came back in their boat. Quek Choo gave them a simple meal of rice and fish and fresh vegetables from her garden.

"Mr. Lim, I thank you very much for your kindness to me," Boon Jin said.

"It's nothing much," smiled Lim Chew.

"I owe my life to you," Boon Jin went on, "yet I want to ask you for more. I want to ask you for a rice bowl: I want to work for you to earn my living."

"Work for me! Your family will never allow it," Lim Chew said.

"My uncle almost drove me away," Boon Jin said. "If he hears that I am dead he will say, 'Better still.' He doesn't want me back."

"Father, we need another pair of hands to help with the work," Chong Beng said. "We can increase our business if he helps us."

Lim Chew had misgivings and it took some time to convince him; but in the end he agreed.

· · ·

Soon after midnight one night, Boon Jin woke and went with Chong Beng and his father to the village a little way down the beach. The fishing boats that had gone out at sunset were returning with their catch. By lantern light, Lim Chew went to each fisherman and inspected the catch. With a few words of bargaining they agreed on a price, and Lim Chew handed over some money.

Boon Jin helped to sort the fish by size and kind, and pack them into baskets with layers of cool leaves between. The baskets were put into Lim Chew's boat which was pulled up on the sand.

Nearer dawn, they set out to market. It was still dark and Quek Choo carried a lantern to light their way to the boat. Boon Jin and Chong Beng pushed it out into the sea and got in too. Lim Chew took up the oars: his crippled leg made him almost helpless on land, but his arms were very powerful. He rowed out from shore.

Stars were white in a moonless sky and the air was cool. All Boon Jin could see was the small yellow light swinging in the darkness, as Quek Choo walked back to the house.

"How to travel in the dark?" he asked.

"Don't look at the light. Soon you'll be able to see," Chong Beng told him. Their voices seemed loud over the creak and splash of oars.

Faint phosphorescence gleamed round the dipping oars. Slowly Boon Jin began to see the outline of the land against the sky. Then he could see smooth ripples on the surface of the water all round the boat, and dawn was coming. Behind them the sky turned red and gold. A gentle wind began to blow. Lim Chew stopped rowing and Chong Beng helped him raise the brown sail. They sailed down the coast, and soon they passed the mouth of the Kallang River; and the city lay before them, green lawns and white towers and spires, shining in the morning sun.

They came in to Beach Road through waters crowded with small shipping. Chong Beng and Boon Jin carried the heavy baskets of fish up stone steps to a jetty and loaded them onto a little cart. Boon Jin looked round for the bullock or pony to pull the cart, before realising that they were hauling it themselves.

Lim Chew went back to his boat. He was sailing back to Siglap to meet the fishermen with the morning catch.

"Come on, Boon Jin!"

Chong Beng pushed and Boon Jin pulled, and the cart's wooden wheels clattered over the brick-paved road beside the black Rochore River. But they were not going to the big market at Rochore.

"We can't sell fish at Tekka," Chong Beng explained, "because it's all controlled by the secret societies. But my father has friends at two markets inland, in the English part of town, so that's where we are going." Chong Beng seemed to have plenty of breath for talking. Boon Jin had got over his injuries, but was only just able to keep up with him.

This part of town was called Small Singapore Beach, in contrast to Big Singapore which was the area Boon Jin knew. It was just as busy, with many Malays and Indians. Chong Beng steered them through the traffic, manoeuvring round bullock carts, staying clear of fast carriages, yelling cheerful curses at rickshaw pullers who swerved in and out of the traffic, and bicycles that dashed madly between the slower vehicles.

They turned away from Rochore River and went down Dhoby Ghaut. Now they were out of the Small Town, among open gardens and playing fields. This was Orchard Road, which Chong Beng called Tanglin Market Street. He pointed out the Hindu temple with a thousand little bells tinkling merrily, and the grand gates of Government House in its private park.

They reached the Orchard Road Market. "Stay here and mind the cart," Chong Beng told Boon Jin. He could see that

Boon Jin couldn't go another step. "What a help it is to have a partner, so that I don't have to worry about leaving the cart!"

Boon Jin had a chance to catch his breath, while Chong Beng carried the fish into the market. He slung the baskets two by two over a carrying pole, and took them to the stall of the fishmonger who would retail them. Then they set off the way they had come, the empty cart banging over the bricks.

They got back to Beach Road Pier and waited till Lim Chew sailed in again from Siglap.

"How is your friend doing?" he asked Chong Beng with a smile. Boon Jin was lying flat on his back in the shade of the cart. "Quek Choo says, don't work him too hard."

"He's as strong as Lu Da in the Water Margin stories," Chong Beng said, grinning.

"Tell her I'm pulling the cart by myself," Boon Jin said, staggering up, "with Chong Beng sitting on top."

Lim Chew had brought their meal cooked by Quek Choo. After eating they reloaded the cart and set out again.

This time they had further to go. They went the same way as before, then past Orchard Market; down Orchard Road, which was lined on both sides with rows of shops and houses, till the buildings ended. They were in a pleasant area of handsome villas surrounded by lush green gardens. A deep monsoon drain ran along one side of the road and on the other side was a Chinese graveyard, where long grass grew over the half-moon-shaped graves.

The brick-paved city street had ended. This end of Orchard Road was made of red laterite earth and stones, muddy and rutted in many places. The cart bumped and stuck, and they sweated and cursed.

"This is a lot faster, with two people to pull," Chong Beng panted.

"I don't know how you could do it by yourself every day," Boon Jin said.

With Boon Jin shoving, and Chong Beng heaving the front end over obstructions, they got over the worst part of the road. They came to Tanglin Village, full of English faces and built in antique English style. They delivered their fish to the Tanglin Market, for what Chong Beng said was a very good price.

They trotted back to Beach Road where Lim Chew was waiting with his boat. Boon Jin slept like a dead man all the way home; and the next day was aching in unaccustomed places, but quite ready to do the whole thing over again.

· · ·

"Buy some New Year food when you go to town," Quek Choo said to her brother one day. "Some waxed sausages, some little oranges. We'll make a little feast to please Father."

"Why not some unicorn's flesh and bear's paws as well?" Chong Beng grumbled. "Where do we have money for such luxuries?"

"I've been saving my money from selling eggs. Here's four dollars."

"My goodness, never knew you were such a rich woman!" Chong Beng marvelled. "Actually, I have some spare money too. Since you've been helping me, Boon Jin, we've got the fish in to market earlier, and got better prices for it. We may be able to get those things."

Boon Jin was immensely pleased that his help had really been useful.

"Buy some cloth then," Quek Choo said, "and I'll sew new coats for you three men."

"What, for me too?" Boon Jin said in surprise.

"Certainly. A good employer looks after his workers at New Year," said Chong Beng grandly. "I'll do the shopping tomorrow; only I'm not sure about how to buy cloth, I hope I don't get cheated."

"I know about cloth," Boon Jin said. "I can do that bit of shopping."

On New Year's Day the four of them sat down in their new clothes to a festive meal. They ate the delicacies purchased in town and one of the fowls Quek Choo reared behind the house. But there was little in the way of ceremonial, no respects to be paid to many elders, no visiting of neighbours or relatives. There were no other Chinese living nearby.

...

"Let's go in the water," Chong Beng said one morning of the holiday, and the boys went down into the warm soft sea. "Hey, Boon Jin, I thought you couldn't swim at all!"

"I can swim, when I haven't been knocked on the head!" Boon Jin retorted. "I used to go in the river near our house, and get beaten for it." His mother, who had thought that he shouldn't let himself get brown and muscular like a labourer, would have been shocked by the way he was growing now. He still thought he would like to be more like Chong Beng.

"You splash like a steamer with a screw propeller," Chong Beng told Boon Jin cheerfully, and showed him how to get better results for less work.

They came out of the water and went to eat. Boon Jin kept wiping off water that dripped out of his long hair.

"Why don't you cut your hair like Chong Beng?" Quek Choo said. "You look so untidy now." Boon Jin had not shaved his head for several days and his forehead was bristling with stubble. He looked at Chong Beng's hair which was cropped level with his ears.

"It would save me a lot of trouble, wouldn't it?"

"I'll do it for you," Quek Choo offered, brandishing her big scissors.

"Go on then. But at home they say," Boon Jin remarked, talking nervously as Quek Choo got to work, "that you mustn't touch scissors or knife during the New Year period, or you'll cut the good luck."

"My grandfather in Java said that kind of thing is foolish superstition—only fit for silly women!"

"That was what my father said, but my mother was very careful about such things."

"I can't be bothered. Now keep still, a few more snips and you're done. There, how do you like that? Neat as a coconut!"

Boon Jin's head felt light. He got up and walked away, leaving more of his past lying with the cut hair on the floor.

...

That night Lim Chew joined the younger people, sitting out on the beach. They sat on an old, smooth tree trunk half-buried in the sand. The white moon, nearly full, rode in the sky and a steady sea wind rustled the coconut trees, and the moonlit waves crashed softly on the moonlit beach.

While Boon Jin was living in Neil Road, he had seldom recited any poetry, even to himself. Apart from the generally discouraging atmosphere, nothing he saw or heard seemed to fit the literary formulae he knew. Chinese poetry was mostly about lakes and rivers and misty mountains, and any scholar could improvise something along the familiar lines. In Singapore town Boon Jin saw bustling traffic, and square stone buildings, and thick greenery of trees left over from the jungle; and the only poetry he thought of was the homesick lament of the princess sent to Manchuria.

But on that night beach at Siglap he found himself happily quoting poems about moonlight and waves. Chong Beng and his father, who had both had a little education, listened appreciatively.

Then Lim Chew started talking about earlier days; and with some urging from Quek Choo, he related how he had first come to the Nanyang.

He had left China when Fukien province was impoverished by fighting and rebellion, and started as a trader in a small town in west Java. Chong Beng had been left at home in China with his mother, but when his mother died he was brought to join his father in Java. Then Lim Chew married a Javanese woman, a widow with a tiny daughter whom he named Quek Choo.

Chong Beng and Quek Choo grew up in the mixed community in the Javanese town, speaking Hokkien and Malay equally fluently. Chong Beng went to the local Chinese school for a few years. Quek Choo didn't go to school but hung about and was indulged by her mother's father: headmaster of the local school, who told her tales of his youth in Jogjakarta.

Chong Beng was eleven years old, and Quek Choo ten, when a terrible fire swept over the town. Quek Choo's mother died in their blazing house; Lim Chew dragged his children to safety but was trapped under falling timber and crippled. He lost all his savings. Friends told him of a chance to make a new start. He brought his children to Singapore and built his house on the beach at Siglap.

. . .

The fifteenth day of the New Year, the night of the full moon, is a special family occasion for Hokkiens. All members of the family are supposed to come home, however far away they may be, to eat the reunion dinner with the family. Boon Jin tried not to think whether his mother would miss him as Chap Goh Meh approached, whether she would cry for him. For himself he was very happy to be with the Lim family.

His old life in Kim Chiam was beginning to seem like a dream. The life he was leading now was so totally different. He did a lot of physical work, and hardly saw as much as a sheet of paper from one day to the next. He had always lived in a big household of many people, all busy with their own affairs. In the isolated house on Siglap beach he had two friends of his own age with whom to laugh and talk. The house and food and clothes were very simple, they were rough compared to the elegant things of home. But day after day there was the dawn breaking over the sea, and the noonday sun burnishing the white palm-fringed beach; and at night waves broke in phosphorescence on the shore.

And Boon Jin thought that perhaps he would spend the rest of his life as a simple fish dealer. In his imagination he talked to his brother Boon Huat. "Brother, please forgive me, that I'm letting you all think that I'm dead. But the family expected so much of me, I just couldn't satisfy them. I want to start out again, without being pressurised by anyone's expectations, and make my life my own way."

There was no way he could even imagine saying this to his Father, but he thought Boon Huat might have understood.

One night Boon Jin dreamt that he was at home in the family Ancestors' Hall. On altars around the long walls stood several hundred wooden spirit tablets, one for each member of the Tan family back into the past. Above the central altar stood the portrait of that great ancestor, who had been the Emperor's Chief Minister.

Boon Jin dreamt that he and Chong Beng were washing the floor of the Ancestors' Hall with buckets of water, and piling up empty baskets that smelled of fish. He showed Chong Beng the altar of his great ancestor. There in the shadowy incense smoke stood the Chief Minister himself, just like his portrait, stroking his venerable beard. "Light the incense sticks," he said in pure classical language.

"Good morning Great-grandancestor!" said Chong Beng cheerfully. But the Chief Minister pointed a long-nailed finger at Boon Jin. "Come here, child. Recite the names of all your ancestors, as you have learned to do."

Boon Jin began to recite, beginning with the Chief Minister, down through the generations and the centuries. But halfway through he looked down at himself, and he was intensely embarrassed to find he was wearing his dirty market clothes. So he hurried away to tidy himself.

The Ancestors' Hall seemed to stretch on and on. Boon Jin saw his mother standing at a little altar in a sunny corner. She was tending the altar, making an offering of narcissus and oranges. On the altar stood a very small tablet only three inches high, with Boon Jin's name on it.

"Mother, I'm here," Boon Jin said, but she paid no attention. So he helped her to tidy the altar and dust the ash away from his own spirit tablet.

. . .

Next day Chong Beng and Boon Jin went into the town of Joo Chiat to buy tobacco for Lim Chew. Boon Jin saw a newspaper vendor, and realised that now he could read a newspaper openly with no one to stop him. He bought a copy of the *Union Times* and when they got back he sat down under a sea-almond tree and unfolded it.

"Oh Heaven, look at the scholar, studying on the holiday," Quek Choo moaned.

"Don't worry: my father says that newspaper reading is just a frivolous waste of time," Boon Jin replied, "so I'm not really studying!"

He planned to read the newspaper very slowly, a bit at a time. He began with the editorial essay, written in elegant classical language on the proposition that the Manchu rulers were just as Chinese as anyone else, being good Confucianists who had upheld all the institutions of the past. Old Eyebrows would have loved the arguments, if anyone in Geok Pin Academy had dared to raise the subject.

"Can I disturb you?" Quek Choo said almost timidly. Boon Jin came back from miles away to find that she was looking at the front page of the *Union Times*. "What do these big words say?"

"That's the name of the newspaper: *Nanyang Zong Hui Pao*." Boon Jin said it in Mandarin and repeated it in Hokkien, "Nanyang News".

"Nanyang News." Quek Choo had been drawing in the sand with a stick. She pointed to the marks she had made. "Hey,

Brother, I've written some words here, bet you can't read them."

Chong Beng came and looked. "What's this, your old rooster been scratching here? What is this supposed to be?"

"Nanyang News," Quek Choo said proudly. "I copied it from the newspaper."

"You copied it!" Chong Beng roared with laughter. "You've no idea how to write characters! You can't learn by copying a newspaper!"

"Why not? I've learned these five words already, haven't I, Boon Jin?"

Boon Jin looked at the marks, which were not much like what his father would have recognised as writing. He said, "Well, don't learn from a newspaper when you can get a living teacher."

"Will you teach me, Boon Jin? Oh please do. I want to be able to read and write. Look out, Brother, Boon Jin is going to teach me, and soon I'll know more than you."

"You think it's so easy?" Chong Beng jeered. "You don't even have any books, or writing pen or paper."

"The Diligent Student wrote with a bamboo stick on the sea strand," Boon Jin quoted solemnly, enjoying his sudden rise to superiority.

"I'll learn to read this newspaper."

"No," Boon Jin said firmly, "one always starts by learning to read the Trimetrical Classic. I will write it out for you."

"Oh yes, the great Trimetrical!" Chong Beng said maliciously, "I enjoyed that one so much, when I went to school." He sprawled on the grass looking as lazy as possible.

Boon Jin made a fuss about clearing a smooth patch of sand. Proud of his firm strokes, he wrote the first four lines of the Trimetrical Classic, which he had learned when he was five years old.

"See this first word, it is pronounced Jen in literary Hokkien. In our everyday language we pronounce it Lang—'man'."

"Jen. That is an easy word to write," Quek Choo said.

"Now repeat after me: Jen chi chor, seng poon sian."

"Jen chi chor, seng poon sian."

"Seng siong koon, see siong wan."

"Seng siong koon, see siong wan. What does that mean?" Quek Choo asked.

"Well, it means something like this in everyday speech." Boon Jin tried to paraphrase those first twelve words. "Man, at his origin—had a soul which was basically attuned to righteousness—but as the influence of his surroundings penetrated his consciousness—his essential innocence departed to a distant awareness."

Quek Choo stared at him. "I didn't understand a word of that," she said. "Explain it properly!"

"I just did! I can't put it any clearer," Boon Jin said.

"I don't understand your explanation," Quek Choo said crossly.

"Well, let's leave it and go on to the next line," said Boon Jin.

"What's the use of going on, when I don't understand the beginning? Can you explain what the next bit means? I don't think you understand it yourself, you big bluffer!"

"Of course I do!"

"Then why don't you explain properly?" Quek Choo yelled. "Do you think I'm too stupid?"

"No, no…Quek Choo, you don't expect to understand the Trimetrical when you first learn it."

"I don't believe you! You don't want to teach me, that's all, you want to make me look like a stupid girl. Well, the hell with you!" Quek Choo kicked sand over the written characters and stormed off.

"I'm sorry…" Boon Jin stammered, completely surprised. "Chong Beng, what's the matter with her?"

Chong Beng got up and went after his sister. "Quek Choo, he's not deceiving you. Nobody understands the Trimetrical Classic…not in the school I went to, anyway."

Quek Choo peeped at him out of the corner of her eyes. "Truly," Chong Beng said. He started to recite the Trimetrical, shouting it out sing-song the way they did in the schools. He hung an idiotic expression on his face and chanted louder, obviously not understanding a word, and suddenly he was using coarse words in the same metre and chanting an indecent parody.

Quek Choo giggled, looking at Boon Jin. He felt offended; he started to get angry, because they were making fun of him and his scholarship. Suddenly he thought of how stunned his father would have looked, if one stood up in the Jade Study and recited Chong Beng's version of the Trimetrical. He started laughing too.

They rolled about on the sand and laughed themselves sore, gasping out rude trimetrical verses. Quek Choo thought of some really wicked ones.

Next day Quek Choo said, "Never mind about your old classics, Boon Jin. Teach me to read your newspaper." She examined the printed pages. "Here's one easy-looking word, what's that?"

"That's 'big'. That one's 'small'."

In a very short time she learned twenty characters. "Now you read something for me, Boon Jin, and I'll see how much I know! Here's a short passage!"

Boon Jin began to read out the article on the need for Reform.

"I can't understand it!" Quek Choo burst out. "What is 'verecundity'? What is 'rejuvenescence'?"

"It means...the author is humble...he says China needs reform," Boon Jin attempted.

"Why can't he say so then?"

"This is literary language, Quek Choo, that we always use

for writing. You don't expect a printed newspaper to be written in the same kind of words we use in everyday conversation, do you?"

"Why not? Why not?" Quek Choo demanded angrily.

"There would be no work for all the letter writers and teachers and scholars," Chong Beng said ironically, "if it were so easy for ordinary people to learn to read and write. So they purposely use an ancient old language and make it difficult to learn."

"Rubbish!" Boon Jin said indignantly.

"I think Chong Beng's right," Quek Choo said resentfully. "How old were you when you started reading that old Trimetrical?"

"Five."

"Hah, and you can't explain it properly now. So it takes ten years of study to understand the first book, eh? How many years before you can read a newspaper, write a letter? I give up."

"You can learn, Quek Choo. I'll teach you a bit every day."

"Yes, whenever you're free, once a year at the New Year holiday, you'll teach me another ten words. How many words are there Boon Jin? Chong Beng, do you know how many words there are in this world?"

"Many thousands, I guess," Chong Beng said.

"Thousands and thousands of wonderful literary words. How far will I get, with 'man' and 'big' and 'small'? Your newspaper is no use to me, Boon Jin. I have had enough of it. I don't want it around."

"Where are you taking it? Hey, where are you going?" Boon Jin was completely surprised by her tantrum, and he was slow in getting up from the sand. Quek Choo had taken the newspaper and run back to her cooking place behind the house. By the time Boon Jin got there, she had rolled the newspaper up and poked one end into the fire. She waved the burning sheaf slowly up and down, just like an old woman burning ghost-money.

"Hey! My newspaper!" Boon Jin snatched at it. Quek Choo danced out of reach, brandishing the flaming paper, and the air was full of smoke and pieces of floating black ash. "Stop it you crazy woman! Chong Beng, make her stop!" Boon Jin managed to corner Quek Choo against the wash tub.

"Got you now you monkey!"

"Let go of me...let go!" Quek Choo bit Boon Jin hard. He yelled and she pushed him away, and ran into the house laughing wildly. He was left with the smouldering remains of the *Union Times*.

"Why did she do that? I hadn't finished reading it yet!"

"Sometimes that girl is a bit mad," Chong Beng said, shaking his head philosophically.

"Some of the articles are all right," Boon Jin said, poring over the fragments. "Most of the editorial is still here..." He salvaged what he could of the blackened pages, while Chong Beng watched him with a pitying smile.

. . .

Boon Jin started buying the *Union Times* whenever he could. He told Chong Beng and Quek Choo about the political issues which had caused such a stir at Geok Pin Academy, and they wanted to hear more, but Lim Chew would not have them discussing such matters in his hearing. "Politics only makes trouble," he said. "We are simple people and these things don't concern us."

Boon Jin's appetite for reading had been reawakened. As soon as he had money to spare he visited the Chinese bookshops in South Bridge Road. Browsing happily there, exchanging literary conversation with the booksellers, he was a scholar again. Volume by volume over the months, he bought a set of the Confucian classics with commentaries, in red cloth bindings. He formed a habit of reading for a couple of hours in the early mornings before starting work.

In those still hours it was easy for Boon Jin to forget everything outside his books. Even the whining insects seemed to be asleep. The whole world was quiet, but for the soft, ever-repeating hiss of the waves falling upon the Siglap beach. He seemed to be listening to the voices of the great scholars of the past, who discussed Confucius with such loving attention. The Classics were not dry to them, but the source of everything they believed in, their guide for every action.

As a schoolboy Boon Jin had studied the Classic Books as classroom texts to be learned by rote. Now he came to understand and value his Confucian tradition better than before.

# 6

Overthrow the Qings, restore the Mings!

*—Initiation oath of Chinese secret societies*

One morning they were returning after market with Boon Jin pushing the empty cart. As he crossed Beach Road a man came suddenly from the side lane and Boon Jin bumped into him with the cart. "Damn fool," the man cursed.

"Fool yourself, don't block people's way," Boon Jin swore back, then wished he had kept quiet. The man pulled out a knife and crouched into a fighting position; his sleeve fell back and showed secret society tattoos on his arm. He was ready to kill Boon Jin for having bumped into him.

But Chong Beng came up behind Boon Jin, brandishing their big chopping knife. Boon Jin grabbed the heavy carrying pole from the cart. He gripped it in both hands and whirled it through the air.

The man ducked back from the sweeping pole. "You be damned, you little scholar," he said to Boon Jin and ran back the way he had come.

"Come on, get out of here," Chong Beng said, hurrying Boon Jin down to Lim Chew's boat. "We're finished if he brings the rest of his gang along. Why did he call you little scholar? Do you know him?"

"Yes, I've met him," Boon Jin gasped, dumping his basket into the boat. "He helped to throw me into the river last time. I kicked him in the guts though."

"Good for you! So that's why he remembers you so well," Chong Beng laughed.

"This is serious business," Lim Chew said. "It's no joke to have the Society after you. The next time you meet that man he'll probably kill you."

"You'd better stay away from the market area for a while," said Chong Beng.

"That man will tell Chua I am still alive and they'll keep looking for me. I can't keep hiding forever," Boon Jin said worriedly.

Lim Chew tugged on the oars. "That gangster saw our faces too," he said. "He may start counting us as the Society's enemies. We won't be safe when we go into town."

Boon Jin looked desperate. "Now I've got you into trouble too. What shall I do?"

"Don't you know anyone with influence?" Lim Chew said.

"The only person who can protect you from the societies is someone high up inside them. Who do you know?"

"My uncle has no influence, or he wouldn't have been frightened of Chua. Anyway I don't want to go back to him."

"Who else do you know then? What about your friend Dr. Lim: a high-up man like him must have influence with the societies."

"He's not in Singapore now; I read in the paper that he's travelling in Java. And he's so Westernised and respectable, I don't think he could have anything to do with the societies. But maybe some of his friends…Do you know who Mr. Khoo Tiong Lay is, do you think he could help?"

"Khoo Tiong Lay!" Lim Chew stopped rowing for a moment. "You know Khoo Tiong Lay? Of course I know who he is. He's the biggest Teochew merchant in Singapore—he's the Big Brother to all the Teochew gangs. He'll be the one to help you all right. Go and see him as soon as you can. Chong Beng should go with you. You never told us that you know Khoo Tiong Lay!"

The wealth of Khoo Tiong Lay seemed much more important to Lim Chew than the civic position of Dr. Lim Boon Keng. If you associated with a rich man some of his good fortune might rub off on you, as surely as syrup sticks to the patrons of the sweet beancurd stall. He went to a lot of trouble to buy an expensive bottle of French brandy; not a bribe but a mark of respect. Boon Jin wrote a little silk scroll to go with it. Next day he and Chong Beng put on their best clothes and called on Khoo Tiong Lay.

• • •

The big house off Balestier Road was called "Thousand Lights House" by the Chinese. Its English name was Tintagel. It resembled a grand French chateau; it had little domed turrets, and a tower with a gilded weather-cock, and a white facade ornamented with plaster wreaths of laurel leaves and flowers.

They were glad to be told that Khoo Tiong Lay was at home. They were brought to a large hall where there were many people who also wanted to see the great man. They waited a long time, under the six crystal chandeliers which gave the house its Chinese name, and Boon Jin's hopes fell. "I don't expect he will remember me," he said nervously. "And even if he does, why should he do anything for me?"

"Just for Dr. Lim's sake, he'll at least say good morning to you," Chong Beng said confidently. "That will give me a chance to speak to him as a fellow Teochew, you know, then he'll be glad to help us!"

Boon Jin did not put much hope in this. The hall where they were waiting was full of Teochews, all hoping Khoo Tiong Lay would help them in some way.

"Khoo's father was one of the first Chinese to plant rubber, along with Tan Chay Yan," said Chong Beng. "He planted thousands of acres near Kajang. Now rubber is selling at over five dollars a kilo and Khoo's the richest man in Singapore."

"How do you know about the price of rubber?" Boon Jin asked laughing.

"Everyone talks about it in the market, don't you listen? Everyone wants to plant rubber, or to buy shares in a rubber company. But it takes money to make money, you see. Who can afford to clear land, and plant it, and wait six or seven years before the trees start producing rubber? You have to be rich to begin with, haven't you? So the rich get richer and the poor stay poor, the world is damned unjust," said Chong Beng, getting heated.

"So how do you expect Khoo Tiong Lay to help you? You don't expect him to pass you one of his spare millions?"

"He might advise us where we could get started. One tip from Khoo might be enough. Just give me one chance and I'll break my back to make the most of it," said Chong Beng fervently.

. . .

"Tan Boon Jin!" A servant called his name. "Are you the one who brought a bottle of brandy for Mr. Khoo? With an inscribed scroll attached to it? Right, come this way, he wants to see you."

Khoo Tiong Lay was sitting in a very European drawing-room, furnished in the heavy late Victorian style; he looked so Westernised that Boon Jin felt he would never understand their problem. But the man with him wore Chinese dress and gold-rimmed spectacles, and he was examining the silk scroll that Boon Jin had written.

"Well, Tan Boon Jin! Where have you been hiding yourself? I haven't seen you attending Dr. Lim's Restore the Emperor meetings lately!"

"I—I was unable to go," stammered Boon Jin.

"I haven't been going either," Khoo Tiong Lay said carelessly. "Now my friend here, Mr. Chooi, has a few questions he would like to ask you!"

"Tan Boon Jin, was it you who wrote this scroll?"

"It's my own clumsy work," Boon Jin replied diffidently. He had practised all morning before writing those sixteen characters: a couplet expressing humble supplication.

"Have you studied the Classics?" the scholarly man asked, and Boon Jin replied that he had gone halfway through Upper Middle School. A few questions followed, which Boon Jin answered easily enough, wondering very much why he was suddenly taking an examination.

"He knows the Classics. But he is young," Mr. Chooi then said to Khoo Tiong Lay.

"The young are more adaptable," Khoo said. "Tan Boon Jin,

didn't I once speak to you about the troubles of China?"

"Yes. You most kindly gave me a pamphlet called 'The Revolutionary Army'," Boon Jin said.

"And do you remember what that pamphlet said?"

Boon Jin remembered it well. The dazzling modern style had stuck in his trained memory, in spite of the unacceptable theme. He began to recite: "Tens of thousands of Chinese were slaughtered, when the Manchus first trampled our land. If our nation wants to be free from the yoke of the Manchus, we need revolution; if our nation wants to be independent, we need revolution; if our nation wants to compete with foreign powers, we need revolution!"

Khoo Tiong Lay looked pleased. Boon Jin went on reciting while behind him he could feel Chong Beng's jaw dropping as he went on and on. When he stopped Khoo said to Mr. Chooi, "Now don't you think this is just the kind of young man we want? Tan Boon Jin, I want you to come and work for me, in a literary capacity!"

Boon Jin could hardly believe his ears. "A literary job!" he repeated.

"For a start," Mr. Chooi said, "I think we'll ask you to be a teacher. We propose to start evening literacy classes for adults: they will learn to read and write modern language, from textbooks that we'll provide. Do you think you can do that?"

"I will try my best and hope to succeed," Boon Jin said

confidently. It was a wonderful prospect and he had almost forgotten why he had come to see Mr. Khoo, till Chong Beng spoke up in Teochew.

"Mr. Khoo, thank you for your kindness to my friend! But we don't know whether he will be safe to carry out his work for you!"

"Safe?" queried Mr. Khoo, and Boon Jin and Chong Beng told him about the gangster's threat.

"We can take care of that problem. Don't worry anymore!" said Khoo Tiong Lay. He introduced them to a hard-eyed man who loafed around the halls.

"This is Elder Brother Tay Joo Eng," said Mr. Khoo.

Tay gave Boon Jin a small, thoughtful smile, as though he were deciding whether or not to step on an ant. "You ran into the Small Dragons, did you?" He beckoned up a very large person who was covered like an ornamental screen with society tattoos.

"Our brother Ah Boey will keep an eye on you and see that you don't get into trouble," Tay Joo Eng told them kindly.

• • •

One morning they sailed their boat past Kallang and Rochore, to the mouth of the Singapore River. Lim Chew skilfully rowed them through the crowded river traffic and they tied up to an iron ring in the wharf; and Ah Boey, the big man Tay Joo Eng had introduced to them, came to meet them.

Chong Beng called a rickshaw and helped his father into it. They started up Boat Quay. Ah Boey walked on one side of the rickshaw and Chong Beng and Boon Jin walked on the other side. They moved along the riverside road, passing go-downs and warehouses. Dockside loafers stared impassively at the little procession of the lame man in the rickshaw, the two younger men and burly Ah Boey with his society tattoos.

Boon Jin parted from his friends near Havelock Road.

"I wish you all success in your new position!" said Chong Beng. "You shouldn't have any gangster trouble now, so come and visit us when you're free!"

"Of course I'll come back to Siglap as often as I can!" said Boon Jin. "And you come round to see me when you finish work." He took his small bundle of clothes and books and walked up towards the Police Court, and caught the tram to Telok Ayer to start his new job.

For the first few weeks that he worked for Khoo Tiong Lay, Boon Jin taught a beginners literacy class. Every evening he faced a class of men who had come to learn to read and write. This was no village class of unwilling peasant boys. These were adults, shop workers and labourers and street tradesmen, who were sacrificing their few leisure hours to acquire an education which they knew was another form of wealth.

Boon Jin could not complain of any inattention. His students watched him with fixed, discomposing concentration. After a while the novelty of the situation wore off, and the students began to get used to the wonderful feeling that a door that had always been closed to them was swinging open. Then they began to feel that Boon Jin was too young to be their teacher. He had not even passed the first government examinations.

The first evening, copying what they knew schoolboys should do, they all rose when Boon Jin entered, and greeted him respectfully: "Good evening, honourable teacher." Later on Boon Jin noticed that some rose reluctantly to their feet when he came in, and the greeting was less than enthusiastic.

He saw how this situation could get worse and end up in a dreadful loss of face for him. So the next evening, he took a deep breath outside the door and strode in saying briskly, "Good evening, comrades!" He was seated at his desk before any of them had stood up. A few scattered voices mumbled "Good evening, comrade," and he got on with the lesson in an atmosphere that had been at least temporarily defused.

But he was relieved when a few days later, Mr. Chooi brought in a wiry greybeard of a former schoolmaster, to take over the class. "Good evening, honourable teacher," said the class with conviction. As Boon Jin left the room with Mr. Chooi he heard the new man demanding names in a voice of experienced authority.

"Come in here," Mr. Chooi said, leading Boon Jin into an office room. "From now on, you're to help me on our newspaper. We're bringing out the first edition two weeks from today; look, this is the masthead." He showed Boon Jin the newspaper's name printed in large characters: *Chong Shing Yit Pao*, with English letters underneath: *Restoration Daily News*.

"As you know, the aim of this newspaper is to educate and enlighten the people and to increase their patriotism," Mr. Chooi continued. "We will publish essays and opinions on political subjects; I have friends here and in Japan who will contribute essays and opinions, and I myself will write editorials. But you see, we must also have some lighter stuff to please the readers! We'll have a couple of pages of jokes, stories, humorous anecdotes—nonsense like that, for the popular taste. You can take charge of that."

Mr. Chooi showed Boon Jin a pile of old newspapers published in Yokohama, San Francisco and Hawaii, and handed him a large pair of scissors. "Look through those, Tan Boon Jin; you should be able to find a lot of snippets we can use!" Anything that had been published was public property, as far as Boon Jin was concerned, and lifting articles from old newspapers was as acceptable as cutting scraps from a pile of old clothes.

Mr. Chooi showed him how to lay out a page. Khoo Tiong Lay had bought a second-hand printing press; the small, spectacled printer who had been brought in from Shanghai demonstrated the laborious process of setting Chinese type. Large rolls of newsprint were delivered at Telok Ayer and the printing press began to turn. The blank paper went into the machine and like magic the sheets appeared on the other side, closely covered with printed words.

Late at night Boon Jin stood gazing, fascinated, watching the press thumping regularly back and forth and the pile of printed sheets steadily growing higher. He saw the page that he had laid out being printed. Down from the machine fell two thousand copies of his work, to be read by so many people whom he had never met. He had a very proud moment, there in that hot cramped office, amidst the smell of newsprint and ink and the monotonous rhythm of the printing press.

Mr. Chooi scanned the damp sheets, inspecting the quality of the print. Boon Jin picked up pages and assembled a few complete copies. He read bits here and there, admiring how the grubby handwritten articles they had worked on now were transformed into sharp black print.

He read Mr. Chooi's introductory editorial. "The aims of this newly-born publication are to promote knowledge among the Overseas Chinese in Southeast Asia, and to enable them to love their race and nation in order to restore Chinese rule in China."

Boon Jin looked at that last line again. "To restore Chinese rule" meant to end Manchu rule, didn't it? Seeing it in print, Boon Jin wondered for the first time whether this newspaper might actually convince some people to fight against the government.

But he had no more time to reflect for he had to get to work, to sort and fold and stack the pages of the newspaper and bundle them up ready for sale. It was early in the morning when they were doing this, but already someone came to the door and asked, "Is the newspaper on sale? I heard that it was appearing today!" That early riser got the very first copy of the *Chong Shing Yit Pao*, which appeared on 20 August 1907. By nine o'clock there was quite a crowd of people waiting outside.

Mr. Khoo Tiong Lay arrived to see the first bundle of newspapers carried to the door. He watched with a satisfied smile as the whole bundle was quickly sold to the waiting people.

"So we have a newspaper to challenge the *Union Times*, and those Reformers will hear our voice! Let's see what Lim Boon Keng thinks of it!"

Boon Jin heard this with some misgivings. Some days ago he had asked Mr. Chooi whether Dr. Lim Boon Keng would contribute articles to the *Chong Shing Yit Pao*.

"I don't think it's very likely," Mr. Chooi had replied. "You should know that Dr. Lim does not agree with what Mr. Khoo Tiong Lay is doing."

"But Dr. Lim runs a newspaper of his own, and Mr. Khoo

is his good friend."

"There are different kinds of newspapers, Tan Boon Jin. And you know, things have changed between Dr. Lim Boon Keng and Mr. Khoo, they no longer mix like milk and water!" Mr. Chooi gave the deprecating smile with which a Chinese gentleman tries to soften harsh comments. It was the first time Boon Jin realised that Khoo Tiong Lay had quarrelled with Dr. Lim. But Boon Jin himself was working for Khoo! He felt that he should try to avoid meeting Dr. Lim.

There was somebody else whom he would probably meet, among the merchants who were Khoo Tiong Lay's associates. He had discussed it with Chong Beng days before, when Chong Beng visited him in Telok Ayer.

"It's going to be rather embarrassing, if I run into my Uncle!"

"He'll think you're a ghost!" Chong Beng laughed. "You're supposed to be dead, aren't you?"

"I have no idea what he thinks happened to me. Yes, I think he'd be quite surprised to see me!"

· · ·

Uncle Tan was among the merchants at the Chinese Chamber of Commerce one evening, as the well-known Mr. Khoo Tiong Lay handed out copies of his new publication. Uncle did not wear his spectacles in public, and naturally he ignored the young man in Western dress who seemed to be assisting Khoo Tiong Lay. But he was surprised and honoured when Mr. Khoo walked over to him and made polite inquiries about his business. Was Mr. Tan interested in promoting *Chong Shing Yit Pao*? Could he perhaps be of some help?

Uncle Tan was only too happy to be of service to the influential Mr. Khoo Tiong Lay. If Khoo was leading some political movement, it was probably wise to stay on the right side of it. In a few minutes, he had promised to help to raise funds and make contacts among the community of rice merchants; and could see several side benefits the task might bring him.

"Good man, I knew I could count on you," Khoo Tiong Lay said, in jovial Western fashion. "Young Tan, my assistant, said that you'd be able to help us; he's some relation of yours, I believe."

Khoo turned away and the young assistant was there, bowing politely; trim and neat, in Western shirt and trousers, with short-cropped hair. "My honourable Uncle, it's a long time since we met. I hope you and Aunt are well? I am so glad to hear that your business is prospering."

Uncle goggled at his nephew Boon Jin, who had been missing since the night of the secret society riots nine months ago. He opened and closed his mouth; the only words that occurred to him were loud and furious ones which he could not say here. Boon Jin covered Uncle's paralysis with polite conversation.

"I fell ill after I left your house, Uncle. I was sick for a long time so I was unable to get in touch with you. Meanwhile, I have found employment with Mr. Khoo Tiong Lay, who has been very good to me."

Uncle was reminded that Boon Jin had just done him a considerable favour by presenting his name to Mr. Khoo.

"So you're working for Mr. Khoo, eh! See that you do well for him! Don't let him down!"

Boon Jin was very relieved to see that Uncle was going to accept the situation. "Please tell my Aunt that I will call to pay my respects, as soon as possible."

"We thought you were dead!" said Uncle. "Old Chua said he saw gangsters chasing you, the night of the riots."

"Chua made a mistake!" Boon Jin said. "It's true, it's dangerous to tangle with the secret societies. But Mr. Tay Joo Eng, Mr. Khoo's friend, says that there's no reason I should be troubled by them."

"You've been introduced to Tay Joo Eng, have you?" Uncle, who was no fool, now understood all he wanted to know. "And you've been lying ill all these months, eh? High time you showed your face to your family," Uncle snorted. "Your parents went through mourning ceremonies for you. Does your father know you're not dead? Have you written to him yet?"

"Can I trouble you to inform him first? Please send my family my deepest respects," Boon Jin said. It was something he couldn't yet make himself do, although he knew that he should: to write to tell his father that he was still alive.

. . .

That night Boon Jin dreamt he was back at home with his family. They were all gathered in the Happy Fragrance Garden near the Ancestors' Hall, eating and drinking, celebrating some happy occasion. Father called for a writing brush and wrote four lines of verse; Boon Huat took the brush and improvised two couplets to complete the poem.

It was Boon Jin's turn, he took up the brush and faced the paper. But somehow Mr. Chooi was there, peering at the paper through his spectacles, telling him something about a sub-heading, and the words at the top of the page were *Chong Shing Yit Pao*. Boon Jin tried to cover the words with his hands, but everyone could see them.

He was standing in front of the big altar in the Ancestors' Hall, and the great Chief Minister was frowning at him. "Useless unfilial son! You bring dishonour to your family. You want to kill the Emperor, kill your mother and father!" Boon Jin stood hanging his head. His ancestors looked down from their spirit tablets all around the hall. Their accusing eyes surrounded him. "Wu zhun wu fu!" they all said together.

There was a noise of shouting and fighting outside. Armed

gangsters were coming down the road. So Boon Jin grabbed a heavy pole to defend himself. He swung the pole in both hands.

The whirling pole struck the spirit tablets on the big altar. They fell clattering among the incense sticks. The pole swept on; the Chief Minister's portrait fell down. The pictures of Confucius and the Emperor went flying. Everything began to crumble and collapse. Above Boon Jin the altar swayed forward. It came toppling down to crush him.

Boon Jin woke up shouting. He was on his mattress in the corner of the newspaper office, amidst the smell of ink and paper, with the printing press looming silent under its covers.

. . .

Boon Jin felt depressed all day. But he cheered up, when Chong Beng came to the office, as he often did when he finished his work. Chong Beng told him the latest gossip around the markets and Boon Jin treated him to a bowl of noodles at a nearby stall.

Then Chong Beng sat around the office, looking at the new *Chong Shing Yit Pao* with great interest. Khoo Tiong Lay passed by and Chong Beng spoke to him. "Mr. Khoo, it's a fine newspaper!"

"Yes?" Khoo smiled, pleased. "What article are you reading there?"

"I am reading about Dr. Sun Yat Sen. But I'm quite ignorant," Chong Beng said with his cheerful grin, "and there are many words I don't know! Boon Jin says there will be night education classes here that I can join."

"Yes, we'll soon be starting a class for advanced readers. You're Tan's friend, Lim Chong Beng, aren't you? You're a fish dealer, with a boat of your own? I have a friend in Malaya who might need your services. He planted a few acres of rubber some years back; now it's beginning to yield, and he's got no way to send it to town. You might go and collect it from him, and bring it to my warehouse, and get a commission for your trouble. It's no great quantity, just a few kilos each month; but if you inquired around his neighbours, you could probably find enough rubber to give you a good boat load."

So as Chong Beng had hoped, Khoo Tiong Lay gave him the first vital nudge to start him towards success. Once a month from then onwards, Chong Beng and his father sailed their boat up to Kelang and filled it with smelly bales of crude rubber, which they brought back to Khoo's Singapore warehouse. Chong Beng was only acting as Khoo Tiong Lay's agent at first; but he took the chance to find out all he could about the rubber trade in the FMS, as people called the four Federated Malay States of British Malaya.

When he came back he sat down with Boon Jin and told him about the little towns where he had stayed, the people he had talked to in the local coffee shops.

"These aren't big rubber planters," he explained. "They don't have hundreds of acres like the British rubber companies. They are just small men, gambier planters, or vegetable farmers or tin mine workers. They happened to have some land, and they just planted some rubber when this great boom began. It seemed like a good idea and didn't cost them much, and they went on with their ordinary work. Now the trees are bearing, they can make extra money by tapping in their spare time. I've got to know some of these men well, Boon Jin, I've got their confidence."

"Yes, so you've made a lot of new friends!"

"See, they each have a few kilos of rubber to sell each month; not enough to carry to town themselves, or for Khoo Tiong Lay to bother with. But all these scraps add up! If only I had money, I'd go round all the small holdings, buy up their rubber—I'd give them a fair price—then I'd sell the lot in Singapore, I'd trade it properly for decent profit! What do you think, Boon Jin? Can't we scrape up capital for just one good venture that would set us up in business?"

"I don't see how we can," Boon Jin said regretfully. "Anyway, what happens if the price of rubber falls? It is going down you know! You could lose all your money!"

"That's the whole idea, buy cheap now, sell dear later on!" Chong Beng said confidently.

"I think you're safer working for Khoo Tiong Lay on commission," said Boon Jin with an air of wisdom. "But look, even working for Khoo, if you had a larger boat you could do much more. I'll give you the money I've saved so far; do you think you can find another boat?"

"I know a man who might sell an old tongkang," said Chong Beng, brightening at the prospect of doing a new deal. He must have mortgaged his father's house and Boon Jin's annual salary, but soon had acquired a sound old second-hand boat to make his next trip to the FMS.

"Oh God, how much have you taken us into debt?" Boon Jin groaned when he heard it.

"Don't worry! Now I can carry bigger loads each trip, we'll pay it off very fast!" Chong Beng said, and by the end of the year they were out of debt.

# 7

> The Reformers are indulging in the futile occupation of trying to revive the dead.
>
> —*Dr. Sun Yat Sen, around 1906*

> The man who dares to plan a revolt in China of today is not a man but a fierce fiend, if he realises all the horrors his diabolical work will cause.
>
> —*Dr. Lim Boon Keng, 1903*

THE BEGINNING OF 1908 was a hectic time for Boon Jin. In addition to compiling the light entertainment pages of the *Chong Shing Yit Pao*, his job was to run many errands on the practical side of printing and distribution. He collected articles from contributors and proofs from printers, carried messages, and organised delivery of the newspaper to the bookshops and reading clubs which distributed it.

At first Mr. Chooi used to tell him everything he had to do. He made some mistakes when he forgot or overlooked important details. There were a couple of times, which he felt very badly, when he unintentionally offended people with his manners different from theirs. Over the months, he learned how to handle people better; he got his work done efficiently, and when little problems came up he knew how to handle them. Mr. Chooi could stay at his overflowing desk in the office, and leave most of the practical side to Boon Jin.

Mr. Chooi relied enough on him to give him extra work not directly connected with the newspaper. During that Chinese New Year, the *Chong Shing Yit Pao* organised a grand public meeting. Mr. Khoo invited a famous orator, Ng Kuan, to come from Japan. This star performer would certainly attract the holiday crowds.

Boon Jin had to make the necessary arrangements. He had to find carpenters to erect a platform on the street outside the office. He had to rent or borrow acetylene-carbide lamps for evening lighting and fix them in high safe places. He prepared piles of handbills. He made posters and ran round town putting them up.

In the midst of all this, thinking of New Year approaching, he wrote home for the first time. He sent his parents as much money as he could, with a short formal letter of filial respects. He wrote a longer letter to his brother Boon Huat, asking how his father felt about his re-appearance.

He told Boon Huat that he had been a teacher for a while,

and now was working on a newspaper. It was the kind of thing that would sound quite respectable to his family. But he was glad that there was little chance of a copy of the *Chong Shing Yit Pao* turning up in Kim Chiam.

On New Year's Day itself, Boon Jin had no choice but to have dinner with Uncle Tan's family, just as Uncle Tan had no choice but to invite him. It wasn't as bad as he had feared. Poh Nam's sniggers and Hock Joo's attempts to show off no longer bothered him, and Uncle treated him with grudging respect.

The day of the speech came. Well-wishers had donated banners with slogans and baskets of flowers, which Boon Jin had arranged around the stage. Crowds gathered in the street and the great orator addressed them. He didn't just lecture; he was a performer who caught hold of their emotions, he made them follow his words and laugh and cry. Mr. Yu Lieh the Chinatown physician did a running translation into Hokkien for the benefit of non-Cantonese speakers. He did it very well, each of his phrases coming right on the heels of Ng Kuan's word; he sweated and shouted and waved his arms, and the spirit of Ng Kuan's message came through him perfectly.

"Equality is a basic right of all people, do you agree? But the Manchus in China don't give us equality: isn't that true? The Manchus are few, the Han Chinese are many: the Manchus rule the Han Chinese, this is injustice, this is inequality.

"Remember the heroes of Fukien and Kwangtung, Zheng

Chenggong, Hong Xiuquan, who fought against the Manchus. Remember that your fathers left China because of Manchu oppression. You Han people living in the Southern Oceans must never forget the sufferings of your ancestors! Avenge their deaths! Revive the patriotic spirit of Zheng and Hong.

"Han people must conquer! The Manchus must die! We must avenge wrongs! We must struggle! Drive out the usurpers! Overthrow the tyrants!"

The audience were the people from Chinatown's streets and cubicles. They had come to hear Ng Kuan for the sake of the free entertainment. Chinese do not like to show their reactions in public so at first they stood stolidly listening with blank faces. But when the orator got to their feelings, they started responding, and cheering, and roaring with rage, just as he wanted them to.

Boon Jin, standing behind the stage, was not enjoying listening to Ng Kuan's speech. He wondered whether this patriotic fervour would last, or whether it would evaporate when the New Year's debris of red paper and orange skins had been swept away and everyone went back to their normal routines. He thought it wouldn't last. He had worked very hard in the last few days and he felt tired and gloomy-tempered.

He reached into his pocket and unfolded a letter which had come to the office that morning, when he was too busy to do more than glance quickly through it. It was from his brother

Boon Huat.

Boon Huat told him that their father was angry. When Uncle sent word that Boon Jin was dead Father had conducted funeral ceremonies, and recorded Boon Jin's death in the family register. Since hearing that Boon Jin was alive, Father had not made any move to correct the records.

"I tried to show him your letter," Boon Huat wrote, "and tell him what you are doing in Singapore. He wouldn't listen. I had to tell Mother about it when Father was out of the room." Then Boon Huat gave the general news of home—the doings of old servants, small alterations to the house and gardens.

It all made Boon Jin homesick. He thought about how the family would celebrate New Year in the ancient, traditional ways, among the flowers and fruit of Fukien's cool season. Here he stood on a dirty street, hot and sweaty, listening to a rabble-rouser shouting treason against the Emperor.

He walked slowly round to the newspaper office; and found Mr. Chooi there with Khoo Tiong Lay.

"Ng Kuan's a success I think!" Mr. Khoo said jovially. "People will be talking about this for a long time! We've done a good service today for the Revolution! You've done well too, Tan Boon Jin," Mr. Khoo added suddenly. "Mr. Chooi is pleased with you. You got your bonus for New Year, didn't you?"

"Yes, I'm most grateful for your generosity," Boon Jin replied.

"I will double it," Khoo said smiling broadly. "And I will

raise your salary." He listened with satisfaction to Boon Jin's thanks. "You've been working very hard; aren't you going to take a holiday for New Year?"

"Mr. Chooi is giving me a week off, when Ng Kuan has gone. I'll visit my friends in Siglap," Boon Jin said.

. . .

The next day was extremely hot; the sky was brassy and glaring, promising a monsoon storm. Boon Jin spent the morning getting the stage dismantled and everything cleared away. Chong Beng came to fetch him, and helped him tidy up.

"Hurry up, it's going to rain!" They sailed up the coast, glancing over their shoulders at the looming black cloud. By the time they reached Siglap the sea was choppy under gusting wind. The downpour caught them as they came in to the beach and, drenched, they raced for the house.

Lim Chew welcomed Boon Jin warmly; Quek Choo, grown a bit taller, brought tea and cakes. Boon Jin handed over a basket of New Year gifts. When he had changed into an old sarong he felt as though he had never been away.

Rain drummed hard on the roof. Lim Chew dozed in his long rattan chair. But Boon Jin and Chong Beng sat out on the front verandah of the house, and Quek Choo joined them with some sewing. The boys lounged comfortably, propping their feet on the verandah rail, and beyond their toes silver streams of water ran from the attap eaves. Below them the sea was grey, streaked with racing white waves; there was a fresh cool wind. Boon Jin told his friends all his misgivings about his job, which he had been unable to share with anyone else.

"I was stupid to begin with," he said gloomily. "I was so happy to get any job using ink, brush and paper—the kind of thing my parents wanted me to do—it never occurred to me that it could lead me into the thick of revolutionary activity! Did you know that last year, Dr. Sun Yat Sen himself was staying at Tintagel for several weeks?'

"What's he like?" Quek Choo asked.

"I haven't met him," Boon Jin admitted. "From the stories I heard, I used to think he was eight feet high with red hair and pointed teeth, but he probably looks quite ordinary really. He's a Western-educated doctor, just like Dr. Lim, and I doubt if he knows classical Chinese. But he's travelled all round the world, and newspapers in England and America print stories about him. So Mr. Khoo Tiong Lay feels very grand, that Dr. Sun has decided to make Tintagel his international headquarters!"

"It really is surprising!" said Chong Beng. "A big millionaire like Mr. Khoo can be Dr. Sun's right-hand man to organise revolution."

"That's what Khoo likes to think anyway! Of course he has the money and that's important. Most of the real work is done by people who have been working with Dr. Sun for years. Mr. Chooi used to run a revolutionary newspaper in Yokohama; and there's Mr. Yu Lieh, the Chinese physician, another old veteran of the revolutionary struggle. I told you I ran into him lecturing on revolutionary theory to Chinatown gangsters."

"Nothing wrong with that, is there?" Chong Beng demanded.

"Well I don't suppose poorly educated people like that can really understand," Boon Jin said placatingly.

"I'm going to start attending night school after New Year," Chong Beng told him. "And certainly we shall study national political affairs. I haven't passed the first government examination. Do you think I won't be able to understand?"

Boon Jin looked surprised. "I suppose—oh, I'm sure you will!"

"Boon Jin, you seem to think that only scholars and bureaucrats can change China by making proclamations and passing laws. But from what I have heard, Sun Yat Sen wants every Chinese to contribute to the new nation. That means people like me too."

"But not me," Quek Choo remarked quietly.

"Oh yes!" Boon Jin said quickly. "In a new society women will be just as important as men. It's part of what Kang Yu Wei taught too: no more foot-binding, women to be free to choose whom they marry."

"Then Kang Yu Wei is as smart as my grandfather," Quek

Choo said. "My grandfather told me that I was lucky to live in Java; if I was born in China, I'd have to have awful pain with my feet being bound. And I know that my mother made up her own mind when she married. But that wasn't what I meant. I keep hearing you talk about restoring the Han people to China. I'm not Han Chinese, am I? Dr. Sun Yat Sen wouldn't want me in his Republic."

Boon Jin stared at her in dismay. He knew that she was Chong Beng's stepsister: he had never thought about her not being Chinese. The question of race had never come up in the little house in Siglap. But Quek Choo just laughed.

"China is far away, and I've never seen it," she said. "Look, the rain has stopped! I'm going to go down on the beach to look for mussel shells."

Boon Jin went to help her. After the rain the firm sand left by the receding tide was stippled like crêped silk; there was a brisk coolness in the air. Quek Choo squatted in her faded sarong, scraping the surface of the sand with a piece of coconut shell.

"Girls like me go to school in Java," she remarked. "My grandfather told me about a Javanese princess, who was just as devoted to education as your people. What was that family quotation you had?"

"'Classic education enlightens minds'. It was written on a board in our Jade Study."

"Princess Kartini died young; she spent her life trying to get education, not just for the children of rich families, but for ordinary ones as well. And especially for girls, because she said that women are important."

And Quek Choo told Boon Jin about Radin Adeng Kartini, the heroine of Indonesian nationalism. "In Jogjakarta there is a Kartini School for Girls. I wish I could go! But I only know how to sort fish and dig for mussels—well, we've found a good bowlful here!"

That night they added the little bivalves, fried with chilli, to their rice.

Next day no one was going to market. "Father, let's make a picnic!" cried Quek Choo. "You know some people living on the islands, don't you? Let's go and visit them. We've got all the food Boon Jin brought, we can make a day of it."

Quek Choo had to work hard to persuade her father to take his boat out on a holiday. But when he had agreed, he smiled and said that he knew an interesting spot among the islands south of Singapore, and he brought them to anchor above a coral reef.

Quek Choo was delighted; so was Boon Jin, who had never seen anything like it before. Chong Beng authoritatively told them to beware of black-spined sea urchins and poisonous fish. They swam about in the clear shallow water, among bright fish and weird coral formations, while Lim Chew meditatively trailed a hand line from the boat.

Then they landed on an uninhabited island. They collected sticks and made a small fire to cook the fish Lim Chew had caught. After eating and resting, they sailed to a village on Merlimau Island, which was Lim Chew's excuse for making the trip; they visited with his Malay friends, and at last sailed home under red skies in the cool of evening.

Tired out with swimming and sailing, half-dazed from the long day in the sun, Boon Jin ate a huge meal and fell asleep in the room he shared with Chong Beng and Lim Chew. He had a dream which he had had before, perhaps two or three times.

He dreamt that he was about four years old and he was playing with a chubby little boy in a yellow coat. They had a marvellous toy, a golden dragon that could shake its head and stare about with its jewelled eyes, as they trundled it down endless corridors. They were very happy together; this was the chief thing that Boon Jin later remembered of the dream, the feeling of going back to an innocent happiness with no idea that it could ever be lost.

After a while Boon Jin's old nurse came fussing along, out of breath, scolding in Teochew-Hokkien. She took charge of the two boys, placed them at a table and fed them with rice porridge.

Boon Jin noticed that the table was oblong, and the stools they sat on were long ovals instead of the usual round shape.

The table and stools all had eight carved legs instead of the usual four, so they had to be elongated to accommodate the extra legs. This struck Boon Jin as funny. He woke up, chuckling aloud, and Chong Beng asked him sleepily what he was laughing about.

It was still very early. Boon Jin got up and found writing materials in his old study corner. When Quek Choo came out she found him on the verandah, reading through several pages he had written.

"Can you listen to this, Quek Choo? I'd like to read it to you: 'Princess Who Fought For People's Education'." He had written the story of Radin Adeng Kartini, in nearly the same words in which Quek Choo had told it.

"Boon Jin that is so nice! Are you going to print it in your newspaper?"

"Oh no. It's in colloquial language after all."

"Yes, I could understand every word! Come on, didn't you write it to get it printed?"

Boon Jin hesitated. "Well…I was just experimenting, to write a whole story in the modern style."

"It was so nice. Go on Boon Jin. You said that Mr. Chooi doesn't interfere with your light entertainment page. He won't mind if you print your own story."

"I would use a pseudonym of course. What about 'by a child from a kampong'?"

"You're no more a kampong boy than Confucius was!"

"But you are, and it was your story after all."

• • •

After the New Year holidays Chong Beng began attending evening classes at Telok Ayer. He couldn't get back to Siglap after the classes and with Mr. Chooi's consent, he slept with Boon Jin on the floor of the office.

"My father approves of me studying," he told Boon Jin, "even if I have to stay away from home most nights. So Quek Choo has to do more work, helping to sort the fish and prepare the boxes for market. She's wild! She says she wishes she could come to town and sleep in the newspaper office!"

"Take this to her, when you go back for the weekend," Boon Jin said, handing Chong Beng a newspaper cutting. Chong Beng unfolded it.

"Princess who fought for people's education…by a child of the kampong! You really did print that story she told you!"

"Do you know, Mr. Chooi liked it very much, even before I told him that I wrote it. And several other people actually mentioned how much they liked it!"

Next time Chong Beng came back from Siglap he gave Boon Jin a little red card. Quek Choo had made her brother write out some characters which she carefully copied onto the card: 'Best congratulations to the famous author, Tan Boon Jin.'

. . .

That little story was about the only article in the *Chong Shing Yit Pao* which really pleased Boon Jin. The newspaper, as he had belatedly realised, was an ideological battleground. Its greatest enemy was the *Union Times* which was published by Lim Boon Keng's group of Reformers. *Chong Shing Yit Pao* tried to persuade its readers that the Reformers were wasting their time, and only the revolutionary cause had any hope of succeeding.

Boon Jin cut out the combative articles which appeared in the *Union Times* and the *Chong Shing Yit Pao*, and pasted them into an old exercise book. Years later this scrapbook was among his papers which his grandson presented to the archives of Wenguang Academy. In the yellowed, fragile strips of newsprint one can read the clanging battle which raged in the Singapore newspapers, for the hearts and minds—and the cash contributions—of the Nanyang Chinese.

The titles of the articles told the tale. *Chong Shing Yit Pao* led off with a gibe from Dr. Sun Yat Sen himself, that "Those Who Fear That Revolution Would Lead to Partition Are Ignorant of World Affairs". In the same condescending vein came "Hearty Advice to Those Who Hope For a Constitutional Monarchy".

The *Union Times* responded with "The Only Means to Save China is a Constitutional Monarchy, Not a Revolution", and an erudite, painstaking explanation, spread over twelve issues of the paper, of why "Revolution is Impractical at the Present Time".

*Chong Shing Yit Pao* replied with a scholarly "Rebuttal of Kang Yu Wei's False Theory that the Chinese and the Manchus Share the Same Fate", and a pragmatic "Comparison of the Simplicity and the Difficulties Between Revolution and Constitutional Monarchy".

"Revolution Cannot be Forced Through," *Union Times* insisted, and "Rejection of Revolution Could Save China."

The debate became abusive: "The Most Shameless are Those Who Hope For a Constitutional Monarchy", *Chong Shing Yit Pao* vituperated, and printed a "Comparison Between Reformists and Prostitutes". Mr. Chooi shook his head and said that in his old Yokohama days, when his readers were expatriate Chinese intellectuals, such debates had been conducted on a high ideological plane.

The *Union Times* replied with equally insulting remarks and sued *Chong Shing Yit Pao* for libel, under British colonial law.

With dismay, Boon Jin wondered how on earth he had ever come to be working for this kind of newspaper. He lay awake at night, wondering whether he should go to Mr. Khoo Tiong Lay and say that he found the work didn't suit him after all, and he wanted to go back to selling fish. When he slept he had bad dreams.

One day in July Mr. Chooi passed Boon Jin a handbill announcing a meeting of the Anti-Opium Society, and told him, "Mr. Khoo says we are all to attend that meeting."

"Since when does *Chong Shing Yit Pao* cover opposition functions?" Boon Jin inquired.

"On some occasions. Remember that affair in Kuala Lumpur last month—when the Reformist group tried to introduce their new Political Information Club?"

"The Tong Meng Hui comrades went along and booed their speaker off the stage—we reported that incident in full!"

"Well, the same man is to speak at the Singapore meeting. He's Xu Chen, one of the old Reformist faction we used to debate against in Yokohama—and no doubt he's here to inaugurate their new society!"

"Now I understand why we're all going," Boon Jin said gloomily.

. . .

There was no way Boon Jin could avoid going to that meeting. Mr. Khoo Tiong Lay did not go himself, but he sent his employees. Mr. Yu Lieh, the Chinese physician from One Leaf House, brought his Chinatown supporters. Tay Joo Eng swaggered in with a group of toughs. They all sat down in a big group together, among the Reformist sympathisers at the meeting of the Anti-Opium Society.

Boon Jin sat down at the end of the row, ready with notebook and sharpened pencil. He felt uncomfortable when he saw the familiar, assured figure of Dr. Lim Boon Keng on the stage, introducing the notable speaker from Yokohama. Since he began working for Khoo Tiong Lay, he had not once spoken to the man who had helped him so much. The speaker, famous Mr. Xu Chen, came forward. Boon Jin began to feel even more uncomfortable as one of the revolutionaries near him called out an insult or two, amidst the general applause.

Xu Chen began by praising the Anti-Opium Society for its work against this social evil. Then he talked about the need for many other reforms in China, particularly in the way she was governed. In this modern age, the will of the people must control the hitherto limitless power of the Emperor: but must work through the peaceful means of constitutional law. For a long time the friends of Mr. Kang Yu Wei and Liang Chi Chao had been pressing the Qing Government to give China a political constitution that would limit the Emperor's powers.

Halfway through this speech, the revolutionary supporters started hissing contemptuously through their teeth. Xu Chen stared over the heads of the hecklers and spoke louder. Dr. Lim Boon Keng, as chairman, rose and walked to the edge of the platform. "I must ask the members of the audience to keep silent, or else leave the hall," he said. They subsided for a while.

Xu Chen looked directly at the group of revolutionaries, and said that all Chinese should work together. They all shared the same pride in their ancient nation and wanted her to be great and glorious as she had been before.

The hissing began again. "Quiet! Quiet!" called back the Reformers' own supporters in the audience. Dr. Lim Boon Keng strode to the edge of the platform and said, "Please let us have silence for the speaker!" He stared at the disturbers one by one and they grew quiet; Boon Jin felt like crawling underneath his chair, as Dr. Lim looked straight at him.

Xu Chen came to the main theme of his speech. Already the Empress Dowager had yielded so far to public opinion, that she had set up a special Bureau to draw up a Constitution. It had stalled for several years. Now the Reformers in Japan had formed a new society, the Political Information Society, Cheng Wen She. Its purpose was to put pressure on the Qing government to finally issue the Constitution and put it into effect.

The revolutionary group, under Lim Boon Keng's eye, coughed and shifted their feet. But Tay Joo Eng stared straight back at Dr. Lim, and spat loudly on the floor. Someone else jeered.

The Reformist supporters shouted back angrily. Tay Joo Eng stood up and stared around him: "Shit on the Cheng Wen

She!" he said. Someone from the audience grabbed Tay Joo Eng, and was knocked across the row of chairs. Uproar and fighting broke out in the hall.

Boon Jin saw Mr. Chooi standing looking nervously around in the chaos. He struggled over and took Mr. Chooi's arm. "You'd better come out of the way, sir." As he guided Mr. Chooi to a quiet corner, Boon Jin saw Dr. Lim Boon Keng urgently talking to Xu Chen; Xu Chen was shaking his head. Next minute, the stage they were standing on swayed and wobbled as fighting men slammed into it. The platform overturned, and crashed to the ground with a splintering of planks. Tay Joo Eng dived into the wreckage and emerged dragging the dazed Xu Chen; and Tay and another gangster started professionally beating the man from Yokohama.

That was what Boon Jin saw, as he pulled Mr. Chooi out of the hall. A whistle was blowing shrilly, to summon help from police or from local gang supporters. It was time to leave; and as Boon Jin stood with Mr. Chooi, anxiously looking round for a rickshaw, Tay Joo Eng ran past laughing like a crowing cock.

. . .

A few days later Boon Jin visited Dr. Lim Boon Keng. He couldn't bear for Dr. Lim, who had seen him at the disastrous meeting, to think that he had helped to wreck it.

He didn't go however to the Philomathic Society, but called on the Doctor at his surgery in the lunch hour. Dr. Lim was reading quietly in his consulting room when the nurse showed Boon Jin in.

"Good afternoon Dr. Lim," Boon Jin said nervously.

"Well, how have you been keeping young man? Come in, sit down!" Dr. Lim said, as friendly as ever.

Boon Jin gave his excuses for his long absence, and explained that he had been employed by Khoo Tiong Lay on the newspaper. "I followed my boss, Mr. Chooi, to the meeting the other night. But I was very distressed that some of the others behaved so badly. I think it was disgraceful, Dr. Lim! I hope Mr. Xu Chen wasn't much hurt."

"He's hurt, but undaunted. But yes, it's a great pity! Even if these people can't co-operate with us, why must they try to frustrate us all the time? Are they afraid that it will be bad publicity for their revolutionary cause, if our petition for Parliament is successful?"

"Well really Dr. Lim," said Boon Jin, "I don't think there's any chance it will succeed! You are petitioning the Emperor, through his Regent, to set up a constitution to limit his own powers. Isn't it like handing a strong man a piece of rope and asking him to tie his own hands and feet? The Government will never voluntarily hand over power to a Parliament."

"They will have no choice in the end," Dr. Lim said firmly.

"The will of the people is a mighty, irresistible force which moves through history. That is the real meaning of democracy. If only the revolutionaries understood this, they would know it is possible to get what they want without violence. The path to democracy is to harness the force of public opinion, and the Cheng Wen She is doing it by asking the people of China to sign their names to the petitions we send to Peking. In Kwangtung, Kwangsi, Anhwei, Shantung, Hunan and Kiangsu, we collected thousands and tens of thousands of signatures. 'Vox populi vox dei'," Dr. Lim said solemnly, "a Latin phrase used by English writers, which means that even an autocrat like the Empress Dowager will be forced to bow to the will of the people."

And Dr. Lim was off, just as in the days when Boon Jin used to come to him for tuition, waving his cigar, his voice vibrant with enthusiasm, as he told Boon Jin about British history and the evolution of Parliament.

After that Boon Jin felt relaxed enough with Dr. Lim to tell him about his job on the *Chong Shing Yit Pao*. "I don't write any pro-revolution articles," he said. "If I were asked to do so I would have to resign. But even the kind of work I am doing now, managing distribution and putting together a light reading page, is still helping the Revolution in a small way. Should I leave that job?"

"Well, why haven't you left already?" Dr. Lim asked in return.

"I feel I should," Boon Jin pondered. "Confucius says that it is cowardly not to do what one knows is right. But Mr. Khoo helped me out of that trouble with the gangsters, and he's given me this good job. And Mr. Chooi, my editor, has been very kind to me. I can't just hand in my resignation one day. It would seem so ungrateful, so insulting."

"Then you mustn't resign. Gratitude to benefactors is also a Confucian virtue," Dr. Lim smiled. "You are right to stay where you are, until you can leave without causing any offence."

Boon Jin nodded, feeling relieved.

"Things might have been simpler, if you could have come to me instead of to Khoo Tiong Lay when you were in trouble! But I was in Java at that time, going round with the Chinese Trade Commissioner. Ah, perhaps this would interest you, Boon Jin! I have talked to the Chinese government officials about setting up a University in China specially for the Overseas Chinese. The Government will provide funds for a college to be built in Nanking. Do you want to apply for a place there?"

Boon Jin thought about it and sighed. "I don't think I can go back to China yet," he said, with lingering regrets for that missed opportunity. But the proposed Nanking College was never built by the Qing government.

Thirteen years later, Tan Kah Kee of Singapore established a University at Amoy for the Nanyang Chinese. Dr. Lim Boon Keng, making his peace with the heirs of Sun Yat Sen, went out to China to become President of the University. But before the Second World War he returned to Singapore, a disappointed man. Under the Nationalists the teaching of Confucius had been de-emphasised and practical affairs mismanaged, and the ideal of Amoy University faded away.

Meanwhile in Singapore, Boon Jin and his wife founded the Wenguang Academy, which taught updated Confucian studies to the Chinese living in the Nanyang.

# 8

> While every son of man is trying to get whatever good is to be got, why should you Straits Chinese remain contented at home? Why should you not go forth and take your fair share of the heritage that belongs to the Sons of Han?
>
> —*Dr. Lim Boon Keng, 1903*

"It's all very well," Chong Beng remarked, "but we'll never get big money like this." It was the end of the day. They were at Khoo Tiong Lay's warehouse near Tanjong Pagar, where Chong Beng had just brought another load of smoked rubber from the FMS. Big Ah Boey had come by in a friendly way, "to see that you're all right", and helped them to unload. Chong Beng thanked him and gave him five dollars.

"We'll never get rich, trading for Khoo Tiong Lay," Chong Beng said. "I wish I had three hundred acres of land up near Ampang, planted with seven-year-old rubber, just ready to start tapping. I tell you, it would be like owning a gold mine."

"Why don't you go and buy a small plot of land then, and

plant it?"

"Because everybody else in Malaya and Singapore is trying to do the same thing. There was a Malacca man who sold his tobacco farm and got some fantastic price for it, from one of the big British Companies. The new owner simply burned off all the tobacco plants and planted the whole thing with rubber. "We'll never afford to buy land, however hard we work, unless we get some stroke of luck!" Chong Beng sighed:

> Big wealth comes by luck,
> small wealth comes by diligence,
> man's legs can only walk,
> but coins roll along!

Boon Jin laughed as Chong Beng recited the proverb. "Let's get something to eat," he said. They walked across to the cluster of food stalls near the waterfront. They sat down at a little table at the edge of the stone wharf: the land was newly reclaimed from swamp, and below them waves lapped on black rocks on which barnacles had not yet had time to grow.

Boon Jin ordered curry and Indian flatbread, for which he had developed a great liking, and coffee spiced with ginger. Chong Beng ordered rice from the next stall.

"I've been studying economics," Chong Beng remarked. "All wealth comes from the land: so it's not fair that a few people should own all the land! When the Chinese revolution succeeds, the land will be evenly divided among all the people."

"Don't talk politics while we're eating!" said Boon Jin. "Since you started going to night school we never seem to stop arguing!"

But Chong Beng was not to be put off. "The Revolution will end China's injustice and suffering," he said earnestly. "In the new Republic everyone will have the means to make his own living, and to help in self-government."

"People's Livelihood and People's Rights. I know Dr. Sun's three great People's Principles," Boon Jin interrupted, "but I only see the Third Principle being preached every day: People's Nation, meaning Han Chinese Nation, Anti-Manchu Nation, Revenge-for-our-ancestors Nation! All right, you can't teach Social Darwinism to the ordinary labourer, so you play on his emotions. The great Revolutionary Army will be just a mad mob screaming for Manchu blood."

"Does it matter, as long as the Revolution succeeds?" Chong Beng asked. "In the new Republic, there will be time to educate the people."

"I hope the Republic never comes," Boon Jin said, half to himself.

"Boon Jin, I know about your ancestors, all loyal to the Emperor for thirty generations," Chong Beng said, "but loyalty need not be blind. Doesn't Mencius say that after all, the

Emperor rules only by the will of the people?"

Boon Jin gazed out across the harbour. The sun was setting, and small waves glinted gold; cool evening mists were gathering round St. John's Island. A fish-eagle soared slowly over the sea. Boon Jin recited softly:

> Who gave the throne to Shun?
> Heaven gave it to him.
> Was it conferred with special injunctions?
> No, Heaven does not speak, only shows its will in his personal
>   conduct and government.
> Shun presided over the sacrifices and all the spirits were well
>   pleased with them, thus Heaven accepted him.
> He presided over the conduct of affairs, and affairs were well-
>   administered, so that the people were at rest under him:
>   thus the people accepted him.
> Heaven gave the throne to him. The people gave it to him.
> The Great Declaration says: Heaven sees as my people see,
>   Heaven hears as my people hear.

"Yes," Chong Beng said. "Doesn't Mencius also say somewhere, that when a dynasty is thoroughly corrupt and decadent as these Qings are, Heaven withdraws its gift? That then it is right for someone else to rule? Then since the Emperor only holds power by the will of the people, why do we need the

Emperor at all! Why not let the people themselves be their own rulers—through the People's Republic?"

"Because without the Chinese Emperor," Boon Jin replied, "the China that has existed three thousand years is finished. I know that Republicans like Zhen Du Xiu want to replace the Classic Books with Marx and Darwin: without the teachings of Confucius, there is no more Chinese civilisation." Boon Jin looked out across the darkening sea, where the lights of ships were beginning to twinkle, and he added: "If the Revolution succeeds you may get the new Republic of China, but the ancient Chinese nation will be gone forever."

. . .

At the Eighth Moon Festival Boon Jin went up to Siglap. Mr. Chooi gave him leave for the holiday. He went up in a bullock cart to Joo Chiat and walked on to the house on the beach. Chong Beng was not there; he had taken the boat up to Johore with Ah Boey, who now helped him regularly. Quek Choo and her father had dinner ready but Chong Beng did not return until well after dark. His small boat scraped onto the beach and he ran up to the house, calling, "Boon Jin, are you there? Listen, we've got the chance of a lifetime!"

Over dinner he told his news.

"There's an old gambier plantation near Batu Pahat which

might be up for sale, cheap. The owner is old and wants to go back to China; and his brother, in Kelang, told me about it."

"Why do you want to buy a gambier plantation?" asked Quek Choo. "Surely you don't want to grow gambier; are you thinking of planting it with rubber?"

"We haven't the money to plant," Boon Jin answered. "But the people who have money, they're hungry to buy land for planting. An old gambier farm should be good well-drained land, and already cleared of jungle; we could re-sell it for a good price."

"It's better than that," Chong Beng said, thumping the table excitedly. "The British plan to extend the railway from Gemas all the way to Johore Bahru, passing close to this farm at Batu Pahat. The owner doesn't seem to know about this; and if he did, he doesn't know the big planters who want to buy estates near the railway. Right now, we're the only ones who know about it!"

"How big is the farm? How much is he asking for it?" Boon Jin asked.

"It's three hundred hectares, and he wants fifteen thousand dollars for it," Chong Beng replied. "We can re-sell it for much more. How do we raise fifteen thousand dollars?"

"We can raise three thousand," said Boon Jin, calculating mentally. "We'd have to get a loan for the rest. If we told Khoo Tiong Lay about it, he would probably lend us twelve thousand dollars."

Chong Beng hesitated. "We already owe Khoo Tiong Lay so much. If he lends us money, we will never be free of our obligation to him. We'll always be bound to him. What about your Uncle Tan, Boon Jin? Could we get a loan from him?"

It was Boon Jin's turn to hesitate. "If we put up three thousand, and Uncle Tan puts up twelve, he's the bigger partner. He'd want a controlling share. And," Boon Jin added, "he's my Uncle." He didn't have to explain to Chong Beng that Uncle, as an older relative, would expect to boss the whole enterprise.

"Who else then?" Chong Beng pondered. "Who else is rich enough, whom we could trust not to swindle us, once we'd told him where it is?"

"What about Dr. Lim Boon Keng?" Quek Choo suggested unexpectedly.

"Yes," Boon Jin said immediately. "Everyone knows he is absolutely upright. Just because of that, he's the director or vice-president of so many companies that if he comes in to help us he won't want to meddle a lot!"

"How soon can you talk to him?" Chong Beng demanded. "We've got to act fast, before anyone else hears about it. Right now we are the only ones who know. Just as you're always telling us, Boon Jin—knowledge is more valuable than jade and gold!"

As soon as they finished eating, Chong Beng and Boon Jin

started back to town to see Dr. Lim. They pushed the small boat into the water. The full moon of China's Harvest Festival made the sky a radiant dome, the sea was like black lacquer painted with gold. Chong Beng hoisted the sail to catch a tiny breath of wind. They sailed through the balmy silver night towards their fortune.

It was near midnight when they reached Dr. Lim's house near Orchard Road, but the Doctor had just come home, in an expansive mood after attending some dinner in town. He insisted on pouring sherry for them and offering cigars, before listening to their proposition.

When he had heard their story he tugged his beard thoughtfully and nodded, as though he saw nothing unusual at being asked to find twelve thousand dollars in the middle of the night. "One-third share to me will be quite satisfactory," he said. "Come and talk to my lawyers in the morning, and then I'll speak to my bankers. And when you have purchased this valuable property, do you know where you mean to re-sell it?"

"Not yet," Chong Beng admitted. "I know that the big British Companies are desperate for good rubber land!"

"That's true. If I tell my friend Mr. Crosfield where he can buy good planting land, near where the railway will run, he'll probably be jolly grateful to me! I'll just mention it to him, shall I?"

Next morning Chong Beng went up to Batu Pahat, haggled

with the owner of the gambier estate and settled on a price which made both parties very happy. When he came back, Dr. Lim introduced him and Boon Jin to Mr. Crosfield of Harrison and Crosfield. The British agents inspected the estate and liked it. One day Chong Beng and Boon Jin went down to the Hongkong and Shanghai Bank, and paid Harrison and Crosfield's cheque for thirty thousand dollars into their own account.

• • •

"We can get started now," said Chong Beng happily. They were eating a celebration dinner at the best restaurant in Joo Chiat town and all of them—Boon Jin, and Chong Beng and his father and sister, and Ah Boey—were dressed in new clothes. It was the strange feeling of his Western suit, with coat and waistcoat and difficult necktie, that helped Boon Jin to realise that poverty was behind them, and a new kind of life was beginning.

Chong Beng had no problems of realisation. He looked dashing in his Western clothes, as though he had worn them all his life; and he was already talking about how they should use their money.

"We can start trading on our own! We'll move into the rubber business, maybe buy some land of our own. We'll politely say goodbye to Khoo Tiong Lay; and say goodbye to the fish baskets too! We don't have to live in Siglap. We'll buy a house in Singapore town."

"Oh yes, I'd like to live in town!" Quek Choo cried excitedly. But their father shook his head.

"I won't stay in the Nanyang any longer. I'll go back to our village," he said. He smiled and spoke the dream of every emigrant, to go back to China after having made his fortune.

"Yes, it's time we all went back to China. My cousins will come out to stare as we ride into the village. Who is this rich man? It's our cousin who went away twenty years ago! I'll greet everyone kindly and invite them to dinner to meet my family. I will build a big house to live in. Perhaps I'll ask the matchmaker to find me a wife."

It was wonderful to feel that hopes were coming true. But the next day Boon Jin found Quek Choo hiding behind the house, curled up in a miserable ball.

"Quek Choo! What's the matter!"

"Go away!" she said, pushing him.

"Why are you crying, what's wrong? Everything's fine now, isn't it?"

"Oh fine! Now we're all going back to China, and I am going to have a new Mama. You heard what he said. Next I suppose he'll be talking about finding me a husband! You and Chong Beng can go back to China. I don't want to go."

Boon Jin didn't know what to say. "Chong Beng and I have to continue working in Singapore. But don't you want to go back to China, see the old country, meet your relatives?"

"They aren't my relatives! They'll call me 'black girl'. I know I'll hate it there!"

Boon Jin remembered how unhappy he had been in a strange country. "But how can you stay here if your father goes back, with no older person to take care of you?"

"I'll stay with you and Chong Beng," Quek Choo said defiantly. But she knew her father wouldn't allow it and she started to cry again.

"I was hoping that if we had some money, I could go to school and study," she said. "In China they won't let girls go to school. I'll probably have to marry some Chinese farmer with a horrible mother. I wish you and Chong Beng never made all that money. I wish we were still poor, and I wouldn't have to go to China!"

Boon Jin had never seen Quek Choo this hopeless and sad. He felt miserable too. Then he had an idea.

"Quek Choo, you want to go to school in Singapore? Would you mind if it was a school teaching English, not Chinese?"

"I wouldn't mind at all. Is there a school I can go to? What are you thinking of?"

"There's this school for girls that Dr. Lim Boon Keng founded, he's President of the Singapore Chinese Girls'

School. He could help you get a place there; and then perhaps you could live at the school, in the boarding house, and that would be all right."

"Boon Jin, can you really get me into that school? Oh wonderful! Let's go and see Dr. Lim today!" Quek Choo jumped up, beaming with joy. "Boon Jin, I've always wanted to learn, and study, and be educated. I want it as much as Chong Beng wants to be rich. I don't think anyone can understand—I want to be someone who knows something, instead of just a stupid girl."

"I can understand," Boon Jin said seriously. "I'll take you to see Dr. Lim Boon Keng, and you tell him that you want to be an educated woman. I am sure he will give you a place in the Singapore Chinese Girls' School."

In the end, the main difficulty came from Lim Chew, who found it hard to understand why his daughter did not want to return to China with him. But with Chong Beng's support, Quek Choo got her way.

Dr. Lim Boon Keng was quite impressed with Quek Choo. For many years, he had been preaching that social reform must start with the education of women, the mothers of future generations. He and his friends had collected money to found the Singapore Chinese Girls' School; Kang Yu Wei himself had drawn up its constitution. But the school was still not popular with the conservative Babas. Dr. Lim was happy to welcome the highly motivated Miss Lim Quek Choo, who brought along a big donation from her brother to help the school's shaky finances.

So while Chong Beng prepared to escort Lim Chew back to China, Quek Choo was preparing herself to move to the school in Singapore town: a journey that would also take her very far from her beginnings.

• • •

Boon Jin was happy that he could now leave the *Chong Shing Yit Pao*. He went to Mr. Chooi and explained that he and Chong Beng had had a stroke of luck, and now he wanted to resign because they were going to set up their own business.

This was perfectly acceptable. It was nothing like saying that he wanted to leave because he had moral objections to what the newspaper was doing. Mr. Chooi shook his hand, and told him to keep up with his literary efforts: "You've been developing an interesting style, in those little articles you've been writing!"

Mr. Khoo Tiong Lay came by and wished him well. "So you're leaving us in order to better yourself, Tan Boon Jin! I am only too happy to encourage your enterprise and initiative." Mr. Khoo didn't seem to mind seeing Boon Jin go. The fact was that lately Mr. Khoo had been feeling his own enterprise and initiative being cramped. Dr. Sun kept sending a stream of letters and instructions to the Tong Meng Hui headquarters at Tintagel. Mr. Khoo's enthusiasm for being just Dr. Sun's faithful follower was decreasing, and so was his commitment to *Chong Shing Yit Pao*.

. . .

Boon Jin hired a carriage to take his books and belongings to Kallang. Near Lavender Street, on a creek of the Kallang River, he and Chong Beng had rented a big shed as their place of business. Chong Beng's tongkang was moored beside it.

Chong Beng stood in the shed surrounded by bales of rubber, which he had brought back from his contacts in the FMS. He was looking forward to selling this on their own account on the Singapore rubber markets, and he suggested again to Boon Jin that they should buy some land of their own to plant with rubber.

"And go hungry for seven years, waiting till you can start tapping," Boon Jin objected. "And do you think you'll be able to sell it then?"

"Of course! In America they are making thousands of motor cars every month, and each motor car needs four rubber tyres! They are buying more and more rubber all the time!"

"Right now, we could sell for better prices than we're actually getting," said Boon Jin. "You know that some of your smallholders send us such poor quality rubber." He picked up a black, smelly lump of rubber, stuck full of dirt and bark and leaves. "Look at this, earth-scrap, rubber-shit they call it on the market! We don't get much for this rubbish!"

"What do you expect?" shrugged Chong Beng. "Those smallholders are only growing rubber part-time; they've got no way to produce beautiful clean Grade One."

"If we were to clean up this scrap and roll it out in sheets, we could sell it at Grade One prices."

Chong Beng stared at Boon Jin. "What great scheme have you got now? You must have been reading inspiring books again!"

"I did read a book on rubber manufacture," Boon Jin agreed. "Look, it's not very complicated to mill crude rubber into good grade. You need rolling machines, which we can order from England; you need lots of water, and a tall building to dry the sheets. The process is not too difficult. Why shouldn't we do it?"

"Let's see how much those machines would cost," said Chong Beng.

By the end of October there was a tall factory off Lavender Street, alongside the Kallang River. A thumping, hissing steam engine turned the different rollers that chewed up the scrap rubber, removed the dirt and pressed it into clear golden sheets.

The last pair of rollers stamped the words "Hock Ha Rubber Company" into each sheet. The English-built machines were sturdy, built to last. In 1970 the iron frame which held the last set of rollers was still doing its job, in the factory run by Boon Jin's heirs.

The milled rubber sheets hung for ten days to dry, over racks in the tall building. It was good brown crepe rubber, called "amber blanket". Boon Jin found that, although the British wanted to buy the best white crepe, the Americans actually preferred the cheaper brown. They did a lot of dealing through Columbia-Oriental Traders in San Francisco.

The work of running the factory came easily to Boon Jin. He was good at grasping all the details of a project and tackling each problem systematically, while keeping the overall picture in his mind. In future years, he would be able to orchestrate the whole complex system that the business eventually grew into. He could have been a very capable Confucian administrator, like his great-grandfather. Chong Beng, no Confucian, was much more of an adventurer; he could easily have been one of the old-time pirates who worked out of Amoy.

Before the new factory started work, while they were waiting for the machinery to come from England, Chong Beng left Singapore for a while. Lim Chew returned to China, and Chong Beng went back with him to their ancestral village and stayed there for six weeks.

Boon Jin did not return to China. He did not feel ready to face his parents yet. Instead he sent a long, polite letter enclosing a big bank draft. He told his parents that he had had good fortune, and would be sending them money every month.

# 9

> The emperor has wealth but he cannot
> buy ten thousand years of life.
>
> —*Chinese proverb*

CHONG BENG WAS in China for six weeks. He returned to Singapore unexpectedly in September, and strode into Boon Jin's office waving a Foochow newspaper. "Have you seen this, Boon Jin? The Constitution that the Government has finally proclaimed!"

Boon Jin looked up from his own newspaper. "Yes: a Parliament for China! The Republicans said we'd never get it! But even the Old Dowager has had to give in at last."

"No such thing!" Chong Beng shouted. "It's another piece of trickery and deception. This so-called Parliament will be completely controlled by the Emperor. He can assemble it or dismiss it as he pleases; he doesn't have to take its advice, he can make laws as he likes without Parliament's approval. The new Constitution is just a sham and a swindle!"

"This is just a beginning," Boon Jin said reasonably. "Even

the British Parliament had to develop through nearly five hundred years, to become the real voice of the people. We'll keep on working, to build on this foundation."

"Work, wait, you scholars and gentlemen are always ready to wait a bit longer! When I went back to China, I saw the people in my ancestral village suffering more than I ever imagined. They can't wait for your slow and gradual changes." Chong Beng walked up and down. The room seemed too small for his indignation, as he told Boon Jin what he had seen in China.

"My father's sister's family was starving. Four years ago the local warlord's men took her husband away to join the army, and she never heard from him again. She and her children struggled to cultivate their land; then the landlord claimed half of their harvest. What was left wasn't enough to live on. Boon Jin, my aunt sold her youngest daughter as a slave, so that she could feed the other children. Before that they had already sold everything else. I couldn't believe how poor they are. They live worse than anyone I've ever seen, almost like animals!"

"Reformed laws and efficient government could help these people!" Boon Jin said firmly. "But fighting and revolution would make their sufferings worse; wasn't that why your father left China in the first place?"

"And you're willing to wait five hundred years, while your Parliament grows strong enough? You're from a rich, aristocratic family, aren't you? You never really understood how the poor people suffer. Now I've seen it. Now I know why even one day more is too long to wait to change China, because every day my aunt and her children are suffering, eating bitterness like rice. No more waiting for gradual change, Boon Jin: there must be a revolution."

. . .

Two months later the Empress Dowager, who had been the great power in China for four decades, died quite suddenly after two days of illness. The news reached Singapore on the sixteenth of November. At the Old Buddha's age of seventy-eight her death was not a great surprise. The shocking thing was that the Emperor Guang Xu was dead too.

The Emperor had also died of sudden illness, just a few hours before his strong aunt who had dominated him all his life. And people said she had had him poisoned.

"What lies!" Boon Jin cried. "What a foul thing to suggest, that the Imperial Woman would murder her own flesh and blood, the child that she always cared for!"

"I wouldn't put anything past that woman," Chong Beng said. "She would have done it out of sheer spite, just to prevent him from getting power at last!"

Chong Beng believed for ever after that the Empress Dowager, feeling life and power slipping away, had ordered the murder of the Emperor; but Boon Jin never saw any evidence to make him believe this.

Dr. Sun, again visiting Singapore, exulted at Tintagel with his followers; but the Reformists grieved.

For years they had been pinning their hopes on what Emperor Guang Xu would do when he finally came to power. Suddenly that hope was gone. There was a vacuum in Peking. A three-year-old child was Emperor Guang Xu's heir. He was placed on the Dragon Throne, with his father as Regent; surrounded by a cabal of Manchu ministers, all more eager to consolidate their own power than to stick out their necks to reform the country.

The Chinese consul in Singapore announced a day of mourning, with traditional ceremonies at the Consulate in Bras Basah Road, and a mourning procession. The *Union Times* published the announcement, and urged everyone to keep shops and business places closed that day, as a mark of respect.

"Of course we'll close the factory," Boon Jin said, reading the notice. "And shall we subscribe to the cost of the procession?"

"No we won't!" exclaimed Chong Beng. "Close the factory? Why should I give up one day's good earning, to mourn for the death of those Manchu tyrants? As for contributions, I'd sooner help pay for a celebration dinner! I'd organise a thanksgiving parade, with bright flags and happy music!"

"That's quite offensive to some people's feelings," Boon Jin said, annoyed.

"Look, Dr. Sun says that anyone who mourns for these oppressors of the people is a traitor himself!"

"I don't agree with many things Dr. Sun says," Boon Jin said, trying to keep his temper. "But Confucius says that a good-hearted man will not rejoice at anyone's misfortune—even his enemy's."

"I am rejoicing at our country's good fortune!" Chong Beng retorted. Boon Jin sighed with exasperation and walked off.

Boon Jin kept remembering how when he was small, he used to imagine that the little Emperor was his playmate. Later, he had had much sympathy for Emperor Guang Xu's attempts to rebel against his elders. Besides what it meant to China, the death of the Emperor struck Boon Jin like the death of a personal friend.

Now another child wore the Imperial yellow, and was called the Son of Heaven. That title still meant something, Boon Jin reflected. The Emperor was a symbol of China's continuity; if there were no more emperor on the throne, Boon Jin thought, China would no longer exist.

. . .

Next day Boon Jin went to the Chinese Chamber of Commerce in Hill Street, where the mourning procession was assembling. In white robes, their official hats covered with sackcloth, stood the merchants who had been awarded—or bought—honorary government positions. There was a long column of school children dressed in white, from schools run by the Reformist group. Dr. Lim Boon Keng had brought the Straits Chinese Association, the leaders of the Hokkien, Cantonese and Hylam communities had brought as many of their people as they could. Every extra person in the procession was regarded as a triumph over the revolutionaries, who had been distributing leaflets everywhere urging people not to close their shops or join the "traitors to Han".

A brass band started to play mournful music. The procession moved out of Hill Street towards Bras Basah Road. At the Chinese Consulate, the mourners would burn incense sticks in front of the portraits of the Emperor and the Empress Dowager, and the Consul would perform the Confucian ceremony.

In Victoria Street the procession encountered revolutionaries who had come to shout and jeer at them. "Traitors to Han! Hypocrites! Pretending to cry for the ones who sucked your blood! Difficult to keep looking miserable, isn't it?" mocked the revolutionaries. "Need help to mourn for the Qing tyrants? Here's some medicine that will make your eyes water properly!"

Boon Jin felt proud of the merchants he marched with. Perspiring in their thick robes, they ignored their hecklers and marched straight on, keeping their dignity.

"Why aren't you crying there?" another voice jeered. "Hey, buy some ointment to make you weep floods of tears!"

Boon Jin saw Chong Beng walking along the line of the procession. He carried a white flag written with the words, "Magic Make-Tears-Come Ointment"; "Come on, buy buy buy!" he was shouting like a street pedlar, grinning widely and enjoying himself. He saw Boon Jin. Their eyes met. Chong Beng faltered for a moment and he walked quietly past Boon Jin's place in the procession, and then he was further up the line and shouting again: "Buy the magic ointment to help you to cry!"

On Dr. Lim's advice, the British had stationed many policemen to keep order along the route of the procession. But elsewhere in the town there was trouble. Gangs of Reform supporters went round and smashed the fittings of shops which had stayed open for business. The revolutionary group retaliated. Street fighting and rioting went on for several days.

The British Governor, who did not much care about Chinese politics, used their own community leaders to calm them. He called up Dr. Lim Boon Keng and Dr. Sun Yat Sen, and got the co-operation of the Hokkien Capitans, and asked them to go round the streets to get their followers under control.

Eventually peace was restored. But the Singapore Chinese community was split down the middle. People had had to make choices and declare their loyalties. So many bitter feelings had been stirred up, that fourteen years later Lim Boon Keng's friend Mr. Song left the whole incident out of the history he was writing. It was still a "sensitive issue", as Singaporeans say, and Song Ong Siang thought it better to make absolutely no mention of what happened on the nineteenth of November 1908.

. . .

One day Boon Jin got a carefully-written note from Quek Choo, inviting him to come to tea. He turned up at four o'clock at the school in Coleman Street.

It seemed this was some end-of-term occasion for parents and guardians to visit the school, and for the older girls to practise some social graces. A proper British afternoon tea was provided in the school hall. Quek Choo hostessed her way very creditably through the ritual of bread and butter, cake, cucumber sandwiches, and tea with milk and sugar.

She liked the school, she told Boon Jin. She was with the small girls in the lowest class, but hoped to move into the next class when school re-opened after the holidays. One of the teachers, Mrs. Marryat, was going to give her extra help. Quek Choo already chattered broken English, very fast; either with the same accent as the other girls or, when she addressed one of the English teachers, with an accent better than Boon Jin's.

Boon Jin asked whether the school had had any trouble during the recent riots.

"No. We peeped out and saw all the shops closed that day. Some of our girls marched in the funeral procession. I didn't want to walk in the hot sun so I wriggled out of it somehow!" laughed Quek Choo. "But the girls who went told us about it. My awful brother went down and made fun of you all!"

"It was a bad thing," Boon Jin said, frowning at the memory. "All right, people have no love for the Qing dynasty—but to exult in the Emperor's death, to make fun of the mourners, that's so mean-minded! You know Confucius says a good man should have 'ren'—should be generous and good-hearted. I hate to see your brother behaving unworthily."

"So have you quarrelled with him?" Quek Choo said sympathetically.

"Quarrelled? Not really. I haven't spoken to him about the matter. In fact I haven't spoken to him at all since that day. If I talk to him we will only argue again, and there's no use arguing anymore."

"I am sure Chong Beng is unhappy that you're not speaking to him," Quek Choo said persuasively. "I expect he was just too enthusiastic, you know what he's like! But I'm sure he didn't mean to offend you. He'll be coming for tea soon. Won't you make friends with him?"

Chong Beng arrived soon after this. He joined Quek Choo's tea table, a little flustered at the unfamiliar social situation.

"I shook your headmistress' hand, was that the right thing to do? She's standing there as grand as Queen Victoria; are we expected to bow to her?"

"Maybe you should, but if she expects me to kiss her hand, I absolutely refuse!" Boon Jin growled, and Chong Beng laughed and the awkwardness between them was forgotten.

Quek Choo talked about her school. "Chong Beng, Mrs. Marryat has asked me to spend the holidays with her family. May I do so?"

"Of course. Dr. Lim said something of the sort should be arranged, you can't spend the holidays in the Kallang factory!"

"Mrs. Marryat's been so kind to me. She and her husband are American missionaries. They have a house on Mount Emily, and during the holidays they will decorate a Christmas tree, and sing carols, and bake cookies and pumpkin pie!" Quek Choo went on. "Will you two come and visit me there? I am sure Mrs. Marryat won't mind. Please do come. She says Christmas is a family time for Christians, and I should have my family to visit me too!"

Somewhat reluctantly, Chong Beng and Boon Jin did visit Quek Choo at the missionaries' house during the Christmas season, and the warm-hearted Americans made them participate in the celebrations much more than they had expected to do. So Boon Jin got a glimpse of yet another set of customs and culture.

• • •

"Would you like to go to the opera?" Boon Jin asked Chong Beng one day.

"What opera do you have in mind?" Chong Beng returned.

"There's a troupe from Hongkong which is performing at the Cantonese theatre. They're very good."

"I'm not too keen on Cantonese opera, can't understand half the words. And I thought classicists like you looked down on popular opera, eh!"

"If you're talking about style, modern writers like the opera just because it is in lively popular language. But the opera is an important way to teach new ideas painlessly to the mass of people," Boon Jin said earnestly. "This opera company, Zhen Tien Sheng, is very good, according to the *Union Times*. One of their plays is about the evils of opium smoking, and most of the money raised is being donated to the Anti-Opium movement."

"Oh, if the *Union Times* says it's good then I suppose we'd better go!"

They arrived early and paid for good seats at the Cantonese theatre in Smith Street. The first play, *The Bell After the Dream*, was the one with an anti-opium message. It was a melodrama during which the audience was asked to imagine themselves now in an opium den, now in a spirit-medium's temple; on a snowy road in a blizzard, and in a white-slaver's brothel.

When this was over the next play was announced: *Xu Xi Lin Shoots General En Ming*. When General En Ming entered, with his face painted to symbolise the wickedest kind of tyrant, he was dressed as a modern Qing official. The brave young hero sang an aria describing the revenge he would take against the Manchu oppressor.

"Come on, let's go home!" Boon Jin said, getting up hastily.

"Oh, let's not waste the money we've paid!" Chong Beng grinned, not moving from his seat. "I'm quite enjoying the show after all!"

Boon Jin strode out of the theatre. Pinned up near the ticket-office, he noticed a list of plays to be performed in the next few days, with titles like *How General Xiung Fei Fought to His Death against Tyrants*. It looked as though the *Union Times* hadn't understood just what kind of social message the crusading drama company was preaching.

· · ·

In its first few months of existence, the Hock Ha Rubber Factory was doing very well indeed. It was a good time for business in Singapore, with the price of rubber soaring to new record levels week by week.

But sometimes Boon Jin felt that Chong Beng was not sufficiently interested in the work that had to be done. He was spending more and more time in revolutionary activities; his trips to the FMS grew longer as he did Tong Meng Hui work in Johore and Perak. When he was in Singapore he was always at Tintagel or at Telok Ayer, leaving Boon Jin to look after the factory.

One day Boon Jin got a call from their bank manager on the newly-installed telephone.

"Mr. Tan, that cheque you have written to Onn Soo Siang—I'm afraid there isn't money in the account to cover it."

"What! I paid in three hundred dollars two days ago. The money ought to be there."

"But yesterday Mr. Lim drew out one hundred and eighty dollars. You come and look at the account yourself."

"Yes. Just hold on there. I'll come down and sort it out."

Boon Jin started making phone calls. Then he called his light carriage and went to the bank, collecting some money on the way from a helpful associate in Almeida Street. He deposited the money at the bank and inspected the Hock Ha accounts. True enough, one hundred and eighty dollars had been withdrawn the day before. Chong Beng had signed the cheque, made out to the Fukien Famine Relief Fund.

"Are you out of your mind?" Boon Jin asked Chong Beng when he got hold of him. "Didn't you remember we have to pay suppliers' bills on Friday?"

"By next week we'll get money from Columbia-Oriental Traders; the suppliers won't mind waiting till then."

"Next week we have to pay the staff salaries! You can't do this kind of thing, just dipping into the cash to make big generous donations."

"Look, you ought to be happy to donate to help starving people in your own province," Chong Beng said heatedly.

"That money doesn't go to the starving, it goes to Sun's rabble of soldiers! We all know Fukien Famine Relief is a cover for the revolutionary fund raising!"

"It's still a good cause! Don't I help to earn this money? Don't I have a right to use it as I think best?"

Boon Jin lost his temper for once. It wasn't the actual money he minded. Chong Beng was endangering the whole business that Boon Jin worked so hard at.

"You! You hardly come near the factory all day, and you give away the money that's needed to keep the business going. When we've got no chemical supplies and no workers because we can't pay for them, then see whether your Revolution will help to feed us!"

Chong Beng blew up in his turn. "You only think of money, you're just a capitalist reactionary after all!"

"Don't quote Marx at me, you village-school scholar!"

"Listen, you great teacher, without me and my father, you'd be reading the Classics to the fish in the sea!"

"And without me you'd still be selling them!"

Words had been spoken that couldn't be taken back. Chong Beng stormed out.

The disagreement about how to spend the Company's money wasn't a small thing. In the end they decided to split up. Chong Beng was rather shocked when Boon Jin suggested it, and called in accountants to divide their assets fairly into two equal shares. But Boon Jin's anger could turn into a chilly determination.

"We disagree too much," he said. "It is better that we each go our own way."

Boon Jin stayed in Singapore, running the rubber factory. Chong Beng took his money, and his boat, and Ah Boey, and went to Penang to continue trading in the FMS.

Boon Jin didn't meet Chong Beng again for a long time.

· · ·

In 1910 Boon Jin went to America for three months.

It was only possible because Dr. Lim Boon Keng asked him to hire a relative of his as foreman at the rubber-milling factory, in which Dr. Lim was a shareholder. Boon Jin was extremely pleased to do any favour for Dr. Lim. Soon he realised that this man, Yin, was an active Reformist worker in China, and presumably was continuing with his work in Singapore. For Dr. Lim's group of Reformers had by no means given up hope, with the death of Emperor Guang Xu.

"Yin left China because the Government was about to arrest him," Dr. Lim explained. "He's an ardent worker for Reform, collected thousands of signatures in Foochow for our last petition."

"Are you organising any more petitions to Peking?" Boon Jin asked.

"Now we can take more direct action," Dr. Lim said confidently. "With the Empress Dowager gone, things are different in Peking. No one faction is powerful: the Ministers who are in favour of Reform can come to the fore, if they get support and finance. You understand that I cannot tell you more about what we are doing," Dr. Lim smiled, "but this time of changes may yet give us the chance to re-shape China."

And once more Dr. Lim made Boon Jin feel that there was hope for China, that through the untiring efforts of men of good will, sanity and enlightenment must eventually prevail.

The man Yin came to the factory and worked well. He was so efficient and reliable, that after a few months Boon Jin decided that he could be left in charge while Boon Jin accepted an invitation from Mr. Fong of Columbia-Oriental Traders in

San Francisco.

"I'm dying with envy!" Quek Choo said when she heard about it. "I wish I could go! But girls can't travel alone. I'll have to wait till I have a husband to take me. You must write to me about everything you see!"

"I will," Boon Jin promised.

He spent three months with Mr. Fong in San Francisco. The large clan of Fong cousins took him about and introduced him to their Chinese-American way of life. He enjoyed a pleasant friendship with the eldest Miss Fong, till she started dropping romantic hints. Then Boon Jin took fright, and afterwards was careful never to be with her without plenty of other people around.

Through Mr. Fong's contacts he inquired into various aspects of the rubber trade in America, which was the main reason for his trip. He visited factories which were being rebuilt, after San Francisco's great earthquake of 1904, to be the most modern in the world. He saw Americans who had come here from all over the world. He saw all the cultures of Europe contributing to the ethnic mix of the new country.

Every morning he wrote about what he had seen and thought and, remembering that he had promised to write to Quek Choo, he sent her these daily observations. His regular journal-keeping became more interesting, as he seemed to be sharing his ideas with someone else. Somebody would have to read the letters to her, but for her sake he kept the language clear and simple.

Quek Choo wrote back thanking him, sometimes asking questions which made him clarify his own thinking. In one of her replies, she asked whether part of his letters could be printed in a local magazine. He assumed she meant a school magazine, suggested that some pseudonym be used, and forgot about it.

. . .

On his way back from America Boon Jin tried to visit his family. His brother Boon Huat came to meet Boon Jin's ship at Amoy, bringing their mother. Boon Jin gave them dinner on board ship and presented handsome gifts from America. Mother was delighted to see him, wiped her eyes and declared she had always known that Boon Jin was a good boy.

Boon Huat said that Father was no longer quite so angry, he had made no objection to Mother coming to meet Boon Jin; but Boon Huat didn't think Boon Jin should go home yet.

Boon Jin asked whether there was a strong Reform movement in the school where Boon Huat was a teacher. Boon Huat looked at him rather blankly and replied, "No no, of course there aren't any rebels in our school! But you've given up all that kind of thing yourself, haven't you?"

Boon Jin said goodbye to his Mother and Brother. From the steamship he watched them getting into sedan chairs and being carried away towards that ancient China which had not changed for hundreds of years.

. . .

When he got back to Singapore in August his first anxiety was to see how his precious factory had got on in his absence— Yin had kept everything running like clockwork.

Then he went to the Chinese Chamber of Commerce. In the yard outside stood three or four gleaming new motor cars, attended by uniformed chauffeurs. Inside, there was a great air of prosperity, and businessmen sitting about looking very pleased with the world. Boon Jin saw his Uncle and greeted him, and Uncle turned round and shook his hand very warmly.

"Hello nephew! How are you? The new factory of yours is doing very well indeed, isn't it?"

"It's not too bad," Boon Jin admitted.

"You were clever, very clever Boon Jin, to get into the rubber business. The rubber price just keeps rising and rising: twelve dollars a kilo now! You must be making a lot of money, eh?" Uncle insisted on buying Boon Jin a drink before letting him go.

Then he went up to Coleman Street and called on Quek Choo, with his arms full of parcels. "Some American picture cards and some candy. Mrs. Fong sent you a fashionable gown and bonnet. And this doll that Miss Fong, their daughter, helped me to choose: it's dressed as a Spanish senorita."

"Thank you, Boon Jin! And thanks for writing to me all the time. I have got something to show you too." Quek Choo produced a copy of a well-known Shanghai-based magazine and showed him a page.

"'Impressions of America'. What's this? My letters!"

"Yes, they were so interesting, with your comments on the American scene; I showed them to some of the teachers and even they were impressed. So I copied the best parts, and sent them to the magazine."

"But you've put my full name on it, Tan Boon Jin!"

"Why not, you're not ashamed of it, are you?"

"No no, I'm delighted, it's wonderful. This is a very prestigious magazine."

"Then you can forget about being so modest and retiring," Quek Choo said firmly. "We're all jolly proud of you! I sent Chong Beng a copy of the magazine too."

"Yes. Er—how is your brother getting on?"

"Oh he's fine, Boon Jin, he's doing business and he's working hard for the Tong Meng Hui. It seems last time Dr. Sun visited Singapore, while you were away, he quarrelled with

Mr. Khoo Tiong Lay."

"I know. The *Chong Shing Yit Pao* has stopped publication, closed down completely, and my friend Mr. Chooi has gone to Penang."

"That's right. Dr. Sun has shifted his whole organisation to Penang, and now Chong Beng is so important in the Tong Meng Hui there."

"I'm sure he is," Boon Jin said and changed the subject.

After this Boon Jin kept busy with the factory and stayed out of politics. But he followed the controversies of the day with interest; continued writing in his spare time, and at Quek Choo's urging sent some articles to local newspapers. Six of his essays were published under the title, "Reflections of a Follower of Confucius on Current Events", and were very successful among the Singapore Chinese. The older generation approved of Boon Jin's Confucian values, though they didn't always agree with how he applied them to current events. Younger people liked the lively modern style of the articles: not for nothing, had Boon Jin edited the light entertainment pages of the *Chong Shing Yit Pao*.

Years later the column "Reflections" regularly commented on events concerning the Chinese of Singapore and Malaysia. In those nineteen-twenties and thirties, Boon Jin avoided making any comment on the chaos which overtook China, under the successors of Sun Yat Sen. Instead he was almost the only Chinese-educated writer who spoke for the rights of the Overseas Chinese, and said that they should be equal partners, in a self-governing country.

After the Japanese War Boon Jin backed the fight for Merdeka. And when Singapore was an independent country, choosing its own rulers, "Reflections" reminded people what Confucius thought a prince should be: that, given integrity and humane feeling, a certain hard-eyed young Hakka might be the modern version of the ideal Confucian ruler.

So Boon Jin helped to shape a country's destiny, as he lay quietly in his grandson's house in Siglap Road; when the years had left little more of him but the clear thoughts and crisp phrases, set down with ink on paper.

. . .

At the end of the year Quek Choo said that she was leaving Singapore Chinese Girls' School. "Mrs. Marryat asked me to stay on and help teach the younger girls, but I told her my brother wants me to join him in Penang."

Boon Jin tried to dissuade her. "Why don't you continue with your studies, Quek Choo? You could even try for the Senior Cambridge Examination. You'd be the first Chinese girl to get the Certificate."

"But what would I do with that piece of paper, Boon Jin?"

Quek Choo laughed. "Frame it up on the wall in my husband's house?"

"Well—then you could go to the Medical School, and become Singapore's first lady doctor! I'm sure it would be interesting. Dr. Lim Boon Keng lectures there too—doesn't take pay for lecturing, of course. The Medical School was another of his great projects. He'd be delighted to have a girl student!"

"Sorry, even for Lim Boon Keng's sake I don't want to be a doctor! Boon Jin, there's no point in my staying at Singapore Chinese Girls' School. Nearly all the girls my age have left to be married, or else they are talking about it. You know, I wanted to learn to read and be educated, so that I wouldn't be just a silly girl. They've been educated, and they are just silly girls who can read! I won't stay at school. I'll go to Penang and keep house for Chong Beng."

"You must go on reading on your own," Boon Jin urged.

"Oh yes. Chong Beng says there's a very good Philomathic Society in Penang," Quek Choo said naughtily. "It's their headquarters for preaching the Chinese Revolution!"

"You always said you're not interested in the Revolution," Boon Jin protested.

"Actually I'm not, so don't worry! Mrs. Marryat says she'll introduce me to some missionaries in Penang who will help me keep on reading. What I would really like to do, Boon Jin," Quek Choo said wistfully, "is to go and study in America, where women go to college just like men. I'd work really hard then."

When the school year ended Quek Choo went up to Penang, and that Christmas was very quiet for Boon Jin.

## 10

> The Overseas Chinese are the Mother of
> the Chinese Revolution.
>
> —*Dr. Sun Yat Sen*

In February 1911 Chong Beng sent Boon Jin a stiff and formal letter. He said that he was about to make his regular visit to his rubber producers in Perak. He suggested that Boon Jin ought to accompany him so that he would know the trade situation.

Boon Jin considered the invitation. He decided that he should indeed get to know the rubber producers; he ought to go, even though he wasn't at all keen to spend a couple of weeks with Chong Beng. Perhaps it would not be too unpleasant if he took care to remain formal and polite. They needn't quarrel again. Anyway it would be nice to see Quek Choo.

He took a comfortable sea trip to Penang on a P & O liner and Chong Beng sent a carriage to fetch him to the house in Northam Road. He was slightly startled to see how grown up Quek Choo looked, in a Western dress with a long draped skirt.

"You look different wearing that dress," he said almost shyly.

"It's what I'm wearing under the dress," said Quek Choo frankly, who had never learned to be shy. She was wearing a corset which squeezed and shaped her into an hour-glass figure, quite unlike the straight-up-and-down figure which a traditional Chinese girl should present.

Chong Beng had invited a few non-political friends for dinner; Quek Choo acted as hostess, chatted politely to everyone and kept things going without strain. After dinner Chong Beng excused himself and went out.

"Another fund-raising meeting, I expect," Quek Choo told Boon Jin, as the other guests departed. "He's been extra busy, since Dr. Sun came through at the end of last year. Did you hear that Dr. Sun got himself chucked out of Penang?"

"For criticising the British colonial government, I read a report of his speech in the Straits Echo. Some Reformists used it as an excuse to get him deported from Penang. His Chinese Revolution isn't aimed against the British."

"Then we'll just have to revolt against the British by ourselves, won't we! Come on, Boon Jin, let's start the Penang Freedom Revolutionary Society, and fight against the wicked white colonialists who get rich at our expense!" Quek Choo struck a flag-waving attitude and started singing the French revolutionary anthem.

"You'd make a great Daughter of the Revolution," chuckled

Boon Jin. "So you have been reading history with your missionary friends!"

"Yes, and some Chinese history too, in translation, that is! And look at this book, Boon Jin. Some professor has translated the Classics into English, with notes underneath. Here's the volume on Li Bo."

Boon Jin examined the translation with great interest.

"Take it along to read on your journey," said Quek Choo.

Next morning Quek Choo saw her brother and Boon Jin off, on the small steam-launch that would take them down the coast. "I think we should meet the merchants at Telok Anson first," Chong Beng told Boon Jin, unsmilingly. They were being very stiff with one another. "Then we should go up to Tapah, and so to Sitiawan—if you have no objection."

"Please arrange whatever you think best," Boon Jin replied equally politely.

The steam-launch was a trim little vessel, her brass-work bright, wood newly painted or varnished. She flew along the coast in the sunshine. Chong Beng sat up on deck, enjoying the ride. "Pretty, isn't she?" Boon Jin nearly remarked, before he remembered that they had quarrelled and shut himself up.

The steamer brought them to Telok Anson at the mouth of the Perak River. It was a large town which had been the first foothold of British colonialisation in Malaya, proudly symbolised by the ornamental water tower erected for Queen

Victoria's Jubilee. Some handsome buildings belonged to the British, others to the rich Chinese merchants; the rest of the town consisted of typical Chinese shophouses, nestled in the crook of the Perak River's arm.

Chong Beng went straight to one which bore a new sign board saying, in elegant characters, "Bei Chih Reading Club". Six men came to greet him. Boon Jin's first impression was that they must be traders or miners; none of them were highly educated; and not one of them had a queue. They seemed delighted to see Chong Beng and extended their warm welcome to Boon Jin as his partner. They insisted, over the usual polite protests, on taking the two off to the town's best restaurant for the kind of meal suitable to honourable guests.

Boon Jin sat quietly at first listening to their talk. They were talking about nationalism, with a strong revolutionary flavour. They might not have had much schooling but he was surprised by their fluency in discussing the important issues. Someone had mentioned Mencius, and Chong Beng was peeping at him sidelong, trying not to appear to be doing so.

"Don't the sages say," said the Reading Club secretary, "that the time comes when the dynasty has to be changed?"

Chong Beng turned to Boon Jin and asked him directly, "What did Mencius say, about a corrupt Emperor losing the Mandate of Heaven?"

Boon Jin was furious. Chong Beng probably knew that

one as well as he did himself. He supposed Chong Beng wanted to impress his revolutionary comrades with his scholarly associate. But although he was very angry he could not let his friend down in front of these small-town merchants, so he recited the passage sonorously. Chong Beng gave him a grateful look.

Then they went on to tell Chong Beng about their preparations for the visit of Wang Ching Wei, well known as a fiery orator for the cause of Revolution. He was to give a talk at the Reading Club in a few days' time, and the Telok Anson men were doing all they could to make it a success. Clearly these people were enthusiastic, responsible key fellows in the organisation of the Revolution, and they seemed to regard Chong Beng as a leader among them.

Towards the end of the meal Boon Jin asked about rubber plantations. Eagerly the men told him about their small holdings. Nearly all of them owned a score or so of acres which they had planted with rubber, during the recent boom years; and they looked forward to the big profits they would earn very soon, when they could begin tapping.

After lunch their friends escorted them to the railway station. "We'll spend the night at Tapah," Chong Beng told Boon Jin.

"Just who are we meeting this time?" Boon Jin inquired dryly. "I hope there's more business for us in Tapah! Your Telok

Anson friends won't have any rubber for us till next year."

"It's always worth making good contacts for the future," Chong Beng replied placatingly, but didn't seem inclined to talk much more. He slept, or pretended to sleep, in a corner of the carriage while Boon Jin read the book Quek Choo had given him, till they arrived at Tapah Road Station.

A hired gharry brought them to Tapah. Boon Jin could see as they went in that this was mainly tin-mining country. There was newly cleared land on each side of the road and acres of young rubber trees, but none were being tapped. They got into the town, a huddle of rough shacks and two rows of shophouses; and Chong Beng headed for a sign board saying "I Chun Reading Club".

Boon Jin followed him, helpless and exasperated. They were given another honorary meal by the officers of the Reading Club, which was another name, Boon Jin had begun to realise, for the local Revolutionary party. The leaders were shopkeepers, small businessmen, tin mine workers with a little money and a little education. This time Chong Beng didn't ask Boon Jin for a quotation. Instead, in the middle of their planning for Wang Ching Wei's visit, he announced: "And I have asked my friend here to give a little talk tonight to the Reading Club Members on the treasures of the poetry of Li Bo."

Of course he had not asked. Boon Jin glared at Chong Beng, and at the pleased, expectant faces turned towards him.

"I'm entirely incapable and unworthy," he said. "But if you all insist..." They did.

He gave his little talk to the audience of Reading Club members, workers who seemed delighted to pick up some of the riches of Chinese culture; perhaps it was a change from the Reading Club's usual diet of revolutionary politics. He didn't have a chance to speak to Chong Beng that night, as after the talk Chong Beng was in conference with the Reading Club officials till long after Boon Jin went to bed.

Next morning the hospitable Tapah men gave them breakfast in the eating shop, urging them to stay on a bit longer.

"We have to get on," Chong Beng told them. "We have to get to Kampar, then Ipoh, Pusing, Lahat. My friend is keen to see them today, if possible."

Boon Jin, exchanging cordial goodbyes with the Tapah people, wanted to strangle Chong Beng. Their carriage rolled up, a closed vehicle where at last they could talk in private, and he jumped in hastily. Chong Beng got up, still talking out of the window to his friends, and the carriage moved off.

"What do you mean," Boon Jin burst out angrily, "saying I'm keen to see a string of little mining towns?"

"Oh, that was just to get us away!"

"I know what you're doing," Boon Jin said hotly. "Rubber-collecting, we haven't seen enough rubber to make a bicycle tyre. You're playing a trick on me, trying to introduce me around all your little so-called Reading Clubs, and get me involved with the revolutionary movement! Getting me to meet people and give talks, making it look as though I'm heartily on your side. Well I am not on your side, and I'm not playing your game! I'll shoot myself, before I let you tie me in with any more of your political organisations."

"I'm sorry you feel that way," Chong Beng said apologetically. "Are you carrying a gun?"

"A gun? What for?"

"You may want to shoot yourself. You see, you're riding in a carriage clearly marked 'Kampar Kai Zhi Lu, Opening-Horizons Association'. They sent the carriage to fetch us; I suppose you didn't see the name when you jumped in."

Boon Jin saw that Chong Beng had tricked him again and he just gaped at him, unable to speak. Then the mild, willing-to-please tone of Chong Beng's voice struck him as very funny and he started to laugh, and Chong Beng joined in with considerable relief. "At least—at least Kai Zhi Lu is a good literary name!" remarked Boon Jin and it set them off again, collapsing all over the cushions of the carriage.

• • •

"You see, I wanted you to see for yourself," Chong Beng said. "I couldn't explain so that you'd understand—that the

Revolution has really become a Revolution of the people."

"I'm beginning to get the point. I wouldn't have believed that simple people like those miners and workers could get so earnestly committed to a principle."

"You wouldn't believe that they could even understand it, you old scholar-snob."

"From what I've heard, I wouldn't say that they do understand all the theoretical background."

"They don't have to," Chong Beng said with energy. "It's enough that they do believe in the idea of the Nation, enough to give their support—their money, even their lives! The people are behind us now, Boon Jin. With their help we can build the Republic."

"I'm beginning to be convinced, Chong Beng. I believe perhaps you do have a mass, popular movement, like the French Revolution. Why did you drag me into it? You still want the prestige of scholarship, don't you; you wanted your peasants to meet your learned partner?"

"I wanted them to meet you, yes, and know you as my partner. Boon Jin, do you know what the French revolutionaries did to their scholars and aristocrats?"

"The guillotine," murmured Boon Jin.

"When our Revolution comes," Chong Beng said, "it may be dangerous to be known as someone who was a Qing sympathiser."

Boon Jin understood that Chong Beng had wanted to protect him, even at a time when they had quarrelled. "I can't agree with your politics," he said slowly, "but I don't mind giving talks on poetry whenever you like! In fact, there's one poem of Bo's that I have been thinking of quite a lot recently." Then he quoted the poem in which Po Chu-I says how much he has been missing his best friend.

Chong Beng smiled. "I like that one. You're a great scholar, as well as a good businessman, Boon Jin! I have to admit that you were right in what you said, about not draining the business. And by the way, I do assure you that there really is plenty of rubber for us around Sitiawan."

True enough, on the fringes of the tin-mining areas, the rubber trees were tall and their planters were starting to tap. Boon Jin got the names of many planters who would be happy to sell their rubber to a Tong Meng Hui comrade. The trip was turning out to be very useful for business, Boon Jin decided, giving himself a good excuse for continuing to follow Chong Beng around.

From Chong Beng's point of view, the main purpose of the trip was to visit and encourage the little revolutionary clubs throughout Perak. As for buying rubber, he left that to Boon Jin. He himself was collecting from each community the funds they had raised to support the Revolution in China. Raising money was what all the action in the FMS was about.

• • •

Tronoh and Pusing, Lahat and Papan are like ghost towns now, old and decaying in a Malaysia where everything important is brand new. They were flourishing tin-mining towns when Boon Jin and Chong Beng got there; and each one had its Reading Club which was a revolutionary centre. In Tronoh the great Min Shu dramatic company had just paid them a visit, in Lahat Boon Jin gave his little cultural talk, in Pusing nobody came to his lecture and the officials of the Reading Club, extremely embarrassed, explained that they hadn't realised that it was the night for a much greater attraction—the Great Zhong Hua Travelling Cinema Show.

Boon Jin and Chong Beng went along to see "The Revolutionary History of Napoleon Bonaparte". The black and white figures, moving with the jerky motion of sixteen frames per second, were projected onto a big sheet in the open air. When the printed dialogue came up on screen Mr. Too Nam, the bespectacled proprietor, translated loudly for the audience. His son turned vigorously at the crank of a gramophone which blared stirring music. The audience loved it and shouted and cheered, and when the hat was passed round, looked willing to contribute.

"Such dedicated people," Chong Beng said admiringly as they went to bed. "Too Nam was a teacher in a Kuala Lumpur school. He's given it up to help the Revolutionary cause. He and his son go round the country, using their picture show to educate the people."

"Watch a film show and you call it education, I still think it's funny," said Boon Jin shaking his head.

"Your ideas need education too," Chong Beng said, yawning. "You still think that people can only learn things that are written with ink on paper, in fine literary language. Those men who shouted and cheered tonight understand well enough what the Revolution is about: they don't have to be able to write one of your Eight-Legged Essays!"

" 'Study without thought is futile, but thought without study is dangerous,'" Boon Jin quoted Confucius glumly.

"Any of these people in Perak would sacrifice his life for the Revolution," said Chong Beng.

One of them did. News came that a Perak tin miner had assassinated a Manchu general in Canton. He became a famous martyr.

His name was Wan Sang Chai—Wen Sheng Zai in Mandarin—and he had worked in a tin mine in Tambun. Just after the Chinese New Year of 1911 he went back to China, and on the eighth of April he was hiding beside a country road in Canton waiting for the Manchu general to pass by. The general had been out to inspect a flypast of brand new, up-to-date aeroplanes, then because the modern age was still barely skin-deep he was carried home in a traditional sedan chair; Wen Sheng Zai leaped out of the bushes and shot him dead. The general's bodyguards, having failed to guard him, grabbed Wen.

Wen was tried and executed. The newspapers were full of his story. He had been a member of Perak Tong Meng Hui, where he was "inspired by stories of revolutionary heroes". He'd seen the opera *Xu Xi Lin Shoots General En Ming*. He told his friends that "he'd decided to follow their footsteps, as there was no other assassin to keep up the spirit of martyrdom". On his way to execution he talked and laughed defiantly, shouting: "I have taken revenge for my compatriots. I hope they will stand up and prove themselves to be men."

Another instant hero, Boon Jin reflected sourly to himself. He remembered Dr. Lim remarking, "It's rather pitiful when a man thinks he can only make his life important by throwing it away." But Boon Jin knew that this was Dr. Lim's Western side speaking. It was part of Chinese tradition, for the country or the community to be more important than the individual.

. . .

"Remember Wan Sang Chai!" Chong Beng shouted, and the audience of tin-mine labourers answered him with a roar. Lantern-light flashed on his face as he waved his arms. "Are you willing to follow his example? Are you willing to sacrifice for the Revolution?"

When Chong Beng read in the newspapers about Wen Sheng Zai's execution, he was so moved that he urged his Tong Meng Hui members in Papan to call a public meeting the same night. He stood on an upturned cart and orated at the audience till he got them thoroughly excited.

"I will pledge loyalty to the Revolution!" a blue-coated worker shouted. "Down with the Manchus! Give me a knife, I'll show my total dedication!" He grabbed a knife in one hand and seized his own long hair in the other, and hacked it off with an air of wishing it was his arm or leg that he could cut off for the sake of the cause. The crowd cheered the dramatic gesture, and others jumped up to do the same.

Boon Jin shook his head sadly, in his place in the shadows at the edge of the crowd. There was a full moon in the sky; serene silver clouds drifted far above the yellow circle of lantern light and the excited meeting.

"Remember the words of our great leader Dr. Sun!" Chong Beng cried. "Comrades overseas sacrifice their money, comrades in China sacrifice their lives! When you see the great sacrifice of Wan Sang Chai, don't hesitate to contribute all you can to the cause." Helpers started rattling the collecting-boxes with a tremendous clatter. People scrambled to throw in their coins, some loudly promised what they would give in future.

Boon Jin turned and strolled away into the night streets. At the other end of the town he found a cluster of food stalls. He sat on a tiny stool at a table, and slowly consumed a bowl of rice porridge and a glass of tea. Then he walked towards the lodging-house where he and Chong Beng were staying. It was near the Papan temple and behind the temple was the local burial ground, on a hill overlooking the valley of the Kinta River. Boon Jin went quietly up the hill under the pale light of the moon.

For fifty years, by then, the Chinese tin miners had been working and clearing the jungle in the Kinta Valley. The country near Papan, looked much as it does now. Boon Jin sat down on a big tombstone and gazed out over the open valley, pale stretches of sand, misty mountains beyond.

Chong Beng found him there very late at night.

"Here you are then, I've been looking for you all over!"

"Hullo, finished rousing the masses?" Boon Jin asked.

"The people are wonderful, their response is so great…Hey, what are you doing up here all alone?"

"I'm composing poetry by moonlight, as a gentleman should," Boon Jin said rather bitterly. " 'The great river rushes swiftly, the waters foam and tumble. The grey heron flies slowly, finding no place to rest in the flood'."

"You mean the Kinta River?" Chong Beng said puzzledly, gazing across the quiet valley.

"Dr. Sun's river, his Revolution. I believe it now. The Revolution will come and there's no way to stop it. They'll establish their Republic and cut off the Emperor's head and all the glories of China's history will be washed away in the floods."

"You do believe in the future of the Republic?" Chong Beng asked uncertainly.

"I believe that it's coming whether I like it or not: this year or next year or ten years more. I won't argue with you any more, I won't stop you contributing your money. I won't try to stop the flood. I'll be the poet sitting in a pavilion on a willow island, watching the river go by."

"Boon Jin, there will be so much work you can do to serve the New China."

"New China? It's got nothing to do with me. When they've slain the Emperor and burned the temples of Confucius, perhaps we'll be able to keep Chinese culture alive in the Nanyang. That's the only work I can see myself doing, for my China."

Boon Jin sighed and Chong Beng said, "You're getting chilled out here in the dew, let's go in." But Boon Jin wasn't ready to leave the melancholy peace of his vigil.

"Look at that scene," he said. "There's the river winding through the plain. And the mountains wreathed in mist. It looks like a classic Chinese painting."

"So it does. Makes you think of home, doesn't it?"

"But it isn't our home. This valley isn't anybody's homeland, is it?" Boon Jin said, philosophising sleepily. "The Malays own it, the British rule it, neither of them work or live in that valley below. It ought to belong to the men who spent their blood and sweat to tame the jungle. But they don't want it, they all want to go back to China."

"And you'd better go back to bed," said Chong Beng, pulling him towards the town. The flickering thought was forgotten. It was fifteen years later when Boon Jin's essays appeared, asserting the rights of the Overseas Chinese in the lands they had opened up.

# 11

> Now Heaven is sending down calamity
> on the State of Chow, and the authors
> of these great distresses appear as if the
> inmates of a house were mutually to
> attack one another. You should realise
> that the Mandate of Heaven has changed!
>
> —*The Book of Histories*

"But how was your business?" Quek Choo asked, after Chong Beng had enthusiastically related the highlights of their journey. "I thought that was the main idea of your trip?"

"So did I," said Boon Jin ruefully, while Chong Beng laughed. "Your honourable brother spent more time talking politics than business, as usual. But anyway he's made so many friends and contacts, I closed three good deals in the Sitiawan area and there'll be many more in the future; all due to his efforts!"

Boon Jin brought out some paper. "Chong Beng, I've got a proposal for you, about our two businesses. Last year when the rubber price was twelve dollars, traders like you must have been singing for joy, but I actually had to go slow at the factory because I didn't want to buy at those prices. Now the price is down to six-sixty, good for me, not such good news for you. What I suggest is, our two enterprises should merge. We set up a proper company with one trading arm, one factory arm. Working and development capital stays in the common pool, extra profits evenly divided between us."

"Merge? That's wonderful! Yes, let's do it," Chong Beng cried, grabbing Boon Jin's hand to shake it.

Quek Choo jumped up. "Oh, Boon Jin! That's wonderful!" she cried, and hugged him in liberated Western style; he didn't know where to look.

"This way even when the rubber price falls, we'll both be protected," Boon Jin said.

"Don't say that," Chong Beng groaned. "Price at twelve dollars six months ago, now half of that, it can't fall any lower!"

"It can, it will!" promised Boon Jin. "We saw a lot of young rubber on our trip, didn't we? What's going to happen when our friends at Telok Anson start tapping, and at Tapah, and at Bidor? What happens when the warehouses are bulging with their rubber, and still more acres maturing every year?"

"But that will mean that rubber will become very cheap," Quek Choo said.

"Yes. Our new company will buy at low prices, and process

it, and at least we make our profit," explained Boon Jin. "When prices are low, manufacturing is better than trading."

"Perhaps I shouldn't have chased him away," Chong Beng said thoughtfully.

"What's that? Chased who?"

"There was a chap in Batu Pahat, wanted me to help him make rubber waterproof boots. I put him off, but I suppose I could get in touch with him again."

"You always know someone," Boon Jin laughed. "Waterproof boots? Well if he knows how to make them we could probably sell quite a lot! Ask him to come and talk to us!"

"We could start by using the present factory," Chong Beng suggested. "Boon Jin, it's going to be great working with you again! Let's go and celebrate."

• • •

A nearby restaurant had a private room for a special meal for the three of them. There was good food and a bottle of fine brandy.

"You know what makes me so happy, I'll be able to give more money to the great revolutionary cause," Chong Beng said. "Just at this moment that's most important."

"Do you have to give your own money?" Quek Choo protested. "You already collected a big sum from the Clubs in

Perak, didn't you!"

"Right now every cent that we can send to the brothers in China is important." Chong Beng lowered his voice. "Listen: we are going to send men and weapons from Penang to start a new uprising in China, which will be the greatest one ever: the one which will finally topple the Manchu government. This will be the turning point. This time we are confident."

Chong Beng told them impressively about the planning of the great uprising. "You know Dr. Sun came to Penang last year. He called a secret meeting in Penang, of the Tong Meng Hui's most trusted, powerful leaders. Even Khoo Tiong Lay didn't know about it. Since then we have been preparing for it. This time we are better organised and better financed than any uprising in the past, and we've got to succeed!"

"You shouldn't be telling me all this, Chong Beng," Boon Jin said slowly. "I'm no revolutionary; how do you know I won't go out and tell all this to the Chinese consul?"

"Because you're my friend," said Chong Beng, flashing his big grin. "You have promised me that you won't let politics make enemies of us. Your old poet was right, nothing is more important than friendship."

Boon Jin couldn't think of anything to say. He patted Chong Beng's shoulder warmly.

"We should go and swear an oath of brotherhood, like heroes in the old days," Chong Beng said.

"Better still," said Boon Jin, "let's be real brothers, brothers-in-law. I will marry Quek Choo."

Chong Beng looked up in surprise and Quek Choo herself stared at him. "Are you serious, Boon Jin?" she asked in a strangled voice.

"Yes: I've just thought of it, but don't you think it's a good idea? It's most suitable for me to marry the sister of my business partner. And as a married woman, you could travel about and see places; you always said that you wanted to have more freedom to move around."

"I did say that, didn't I? How considerate you are! Do I have any choice about it?"

"Of course," Boon Jin said, shocked. "We are modern people. Your father or brother will not choose for you. You choose for yourself, and I am asking you."

"But why are you asking me? Maybe you won't feel the same way tomorrow! Let me think about it, Boon Jin; and tomorrow, if you haven't changed your mind, you ask me again."

After Quek Choo went to bed, Boon Jin and Chong Beng sat up and finished the bottle of brandy, drinking to their friendship and their business partnership and quite a few other things. Chong Beng's face glowed deep red and he got very cheerful, Boon Jin went extremely pale and solemn. But he was quite sure that he had not been drunk when he asked Quek Choo to marry him.

Next day he saw Quek Choo and Chong Beng again.

"Boon Jin, I've thought about what you said. I think that as far as getting more freedom is concerned, I would do better to marry one of the Straits Chinese boys instead."

Boon Jin and Chong Beng both protested loudly.

"Nothing personal, Boon Jin; it's just that you do have these old-fashioned ideas, and you'd expect me to be a good Confucian wife all the time."

"Absolutely not, Quek Choo. You don't have to stay at home; you can go out, mix about as much as you want."

"Brother, you heard what he said, you're a witness. No second wives or concubines, Boon Jin?"

"No no no!" Boon Jin was getting flustered. "Complete equality between husband and wife. Same rules of good behaviour apply to you and to me."

"Brother, you're a witness. But what about your family in China, Boon Jin? They won't approve of me as a suitable daughter-in-law. Your father will never consent."

"I am not asking for his consent. I have made up my mind," Boon Jin said firmly. "We will be married in Singapore at the Registry office in the modern way, and we won't need any traditional family ceremonies. My father can't stop me from marrying you if I want to."

"You're quite sure you want to? Even though I am so unsuitable?"

"You are the most suitable wife I could have, being the sister of my business partner. Quek Choo, wouldn't you like to marry me? We've always been good friends and got along so well together."

"Of course you will, won't you, sister!" chipped in Chong Beng. "Boon Jin will give you a very comfortable life and you can travel, do all those things you wanted to do. He's the best husband I could ever find for you!"

"Yes, all right, I'll marry you Boon Jin!"

• • •

Boon Jin wrote to tell his parents that he was marrying Quek Choo, explaining that she had few relatives and there would be no formal exchange of gifts with her family. "They'll be furious, but I'm not waiting till they pick out some bride for me!" He was touched and surprised when his mother sent Quek Choo a jade bracelet and a brocade coat. Boon Huat sent him a pair of carved name seals, joined together with scarlet cord.

Quek Choo's father sent his blessings from China. Uncle Tan, having decided to approve of Boon Jin, presented some heavy silver tableware and brought all the aunts and cousins to the wedding, making it quite a family occasion after all. Dr. Lim Boon Keng gave away the bride.

"I'm happy to have seen your wedding, before I leave Singapore," Dr. Lim told Boon Jin during the dinner party.

"I understand you'll be in Europe for quite a long time, sir?"

"I have several official duties to perform. I am travelling with the Imperial Chinese Commission to the International Hygiene Exhibition, as China's Medical Delegate there. And then there is a great international meeting in London, the First Universal Races Conference." Dr. Lim shook his head gravely. "War clouds are gathering in Europe. I hope this great multi-racial gathering can be a force for peace!"

"You'll be representing China there too?" asked Boon Jin.

"I have been given that honour. In fact in London I shall be officially acting as a Secretary of the Chinese Legation. The Minister of the Interior seems to value my knowledge of the West. Doesn't this prove, Tan Boon Jin, that at least one Manchu Minister is enlightened and progressive?"

Boon Jin glanced to see whether Chong Beng had heard. But Chong Beng was not listening. He had been best man at the wedding, but had been rather absent-minded all day: he was waiting to hear news from China. Boon Jin knew that throughout the past week, scores of boats and junks had sailed secretly for ports around Canton; filled with trained secret society fighters, and keen volunteers from Singapore and the FMS, to join the great uprising that was being planned.

• • •

The great Canton Rebellion in the third month of 1911 was another failure. The revolutionary fighters were defeated by the Chinese government's soldiers and those who survived ran to their boats, and fled out again from China. Disheartened and penniless, they flooded into Singapore.

Khoo Tiong Lay spent a lot of money to look after these men: he helped them, clothed them, found them jobs wherever possible. Perhaps he didn't exactly rejoice that this uprising of Dr. Sun's had failed: but he certainly gained a lot of face, by succouring the men who had followed Sun Yat Sen.

Boon Jin's uncle called on him one day and when polite conversation was over, explained that he was having trouble at the rice warehouse. It had been virtually taken over by gangsters from China, who were heads of old Chua's Small Dragon Society. Thirty or forty men were using the warehouse as their living-place, sleeping among the sacks of rice, feeding themselves from the stocks, and getting pocket money by selling an occasional sack of rice to local shopkeepers.

Boon Jin said he would do what he could to help. He took Uncle to call on Khoo Tiong Lay. Later that day Tay Joo Eng himself went down to the warehouse. The gangsters from China received him politely, and he gave them Mr. Khoo's invitation to move into a large house in Pasir Panjang, and later to go up to jobs in the FMS. Most of the money to finance this was Uncle's: the prestige which persuaded the gangsters to move was Mr. Khoo's.

Boon Jin stood behind Tay Joo Eng as he negotiated with the Small Dragon leader. He saw old Chua sitting in a corner, being ignored by the men from China in his own warehouse. He could only look on as their leader did the talking. He hadn't been able to do a thing to control them. He had had to wait till Tay Joo Eng came to the rescue, and it was Boon Jin who had brought Tay Joo Eng along.

Boon Jin met old Chua's eyes, and nodded once. He said nothing; he didn't have to. Next morning the men from China were gone from the warehouse, and so was old Chua.

. . .

"The country is peaceful right now," said Boon Jin. "There's no danger, it's a good time for me to take Quek Choo back to meet my family. Anyone planning any more revolutions? You ought to know!"

Chong Beng shook his head glumly. He was temporarily very discouraged by the failure of the Canton Uprising. He did not object, when Boon Jin and Quek Choo boarded a ship to visit Boon Jin's home near Kim Chiam.

Amoy was full of soldiers. The local governor had tripled his personal guards and was making his island into a fortress, as it had been in the past.

Rocky Amoy island on the Pearl River used to be called "Se-Ming"—which meant "remember the Mings", the war cry of anti-Manchu rebels. In the seventeenth century it was the headquarters of the freedom-fighter Zheng Chenggong, whom the Portuguese called Koxinga. Later all sorts of pirates used its broad harbour to make lightning raids on the mainland, then disappear over the horizon to Taiwan or Macao. It was rebel country; and if the Central Government should fall, and chaos should overwhelm the mainland, the governor was prepared to break away and make Amoy once more an independent stronghold.

Boon Jin was told that the roads were dangerous for a small party. He joined a party of merchants travelling together, with a large company of soldiers to guard them.

"I didn't anticipate going back in quite so much style as this," he said to Quek Choo.

"We need the soldiers for protection; but you don't have to hire a sedan chair for me. I would prefer to ride in the cart; it makes me uncomfortable to have men struggling to carry me."

"Don't be so English-educated," Boon Jin said ironically. "How will my family know that you're the wife of someone important, if you don't make other people suffer?"

His own feelings were confused. He saw familiar scenes again, just as they had been preserved in bright childhood memories; but at the same time he noticed dirt and poverty and hardship.

"I'd forgotten these things about China," he told Quek Choo. "Or perhaps I didn't notice, when I was younger."

"No wonder my father emigrated to the Nanyang!"

Their company of armed men was enough to protect them from attacks by most of the poor, ragged bandits roaming the country—mainly defeated rebels or farmers whose fields had been burned. But towards evening they met a troop of well-armed, uniformed soldiers who ordered them to stop.

Boon Jin showed the leader their papers, adding, "We are going towards Kim Chiam, as friends of Magistrate Pu."

"Magistrate Your-father's-head," sneered the leader, unimpressed. But when he looked at Quek Choo's British passport, issued by the Governor of Singapore, his manner changed and he became much more polite. "You may go on," he said, "on payment of a fee of ten dollars each to my Master who protects this part of the country."

Boon Jin paid up promptly, glad it was no more. "Who is your Master?" he inquired. "I'll visit him to pay my respects."

"Our master is General Jun," the soldier informed him. General Jun was a warlord from a district thirty miles away; he must be expanding the area under his control.

They left Kim Chiam town behind and presently Boon Jin left his own sedan chair and walked. "This is our family burying-ground," he told Quek Choo. "I have to show some respect for the ancestors." So he came on foot back to his ancestral home, followed by the little procession of armed men and sedan chairs and men bearing gifts.

His parents met him in the centre court, treating him like an honoured visitor. The gifts were presented, modern Western gadgets and Southern food delicacies such as bird's nest and shark's fin. Boon Jin and Quek Choo went through formal ceremonies of pouring tea for the parents, and offering incense in the Ancestors' Hall.

. . .

Boon Jin had hoped his mother would like Quek Choo, but she and her daughter-in-law, Boon Huat's wife, were unfriendly to her. They whispered to each other, looking at her unbound feet and giggling.

"I'm sorry they aren't being good to you!" Boon Jin apologised to Quek Choo in private. "It is difficult coming to a new place, I was miserable too when I first came to the Nanyang."

"I can learn their ways and get used to them; but the trouble is your mother doesn't like me because I am not Chinese. She thinks I can't produce proper Chinese grandsons to make offerings to her spirit."

Boon Jin was silent. He recognised a deep root of Chinese chauvinism, for which there could be no cure till people stopped seriously believing in the rites of sacrifice to ancestral spirits.

"I'm glad we came, Boon Jin. Now I understand more about your family. I've seen your Ancestors' Hall, and the graveyard where thirty generations of Tans have been buried. Even the village people know their families have been here for hundreds and hundreds of years. But I don't have any grandfather buried here. I'll never belong, even if I live here for sixty years and produce ten sons."

And the next day Quek Choo put on her Western dress, stockings and fashionable shoes. "From now on I'll just be the barbarian visitor, not some kind of imitation Chinese," she said, and Mother seemed to be more comfortable with her like that.

This problem didn't arise with Father, because he didn't talk to women anyway. But he sat down to talk to Boon Jin, who told him about the soldiers of General Jun who had stopped them on their way.

"General Jun he calls himself!" Father said scornfully, "He holds no commission from the Emperor, he is nothing but a ruffian who has gathered soldiers and set up his own private army."

"Do you know him, Father? Have you visited him?"

"I see no reason to visit him. He is a man of no culture and no legal authority. He is little better than one of those damned rebels, himself."

"Father, as long as he's the big power around here, it might be better to be under his protection."

"Why do we need protection? Magistrate Pu is my friend; that's good enough!"

"Father, Magistrate Pu doesn't have many soldiers. The fact is that the friendship of the Manchus may be more dangerous than helpful."

"What do you mean?"

"I mean that if a troop of revolutionaries comes to the house, they won't be frightened if you mention Magistrate Pu's name: they are more likely to burn your house down because you're his friend. You'd be safer if you could tell them that General Jun was protecting you. Or else," Boon Jin said, being sarcastic again, "you can keep a portrait of Sun Yat Sen in the house, and wave it at the revolutionaries!"

"Pretend to be a supporter of that devil, Sun? I'd rather die!" Father shouted. "So you're a rebel still, are you! A traitor to your country, disloyal to all your ancestors who served the Emperor!"

"Father, 'Heaven and earth exist forever, mountains and rivers never change', but man's existence is impermanent."

Father paused to listen to the literary language.

"When the dynasty is corrupt it loses the favour of Heaven. But China is more than the Qing dynasty—it is more than the Emperor's throne. As long as the people respect the teachings of Confucius, and read the poets, and remember Chinese history, the soul of China will survive."

And Boon Jin tried to tell Father the ideas he had slowly reached.

"Chinese culture and identity can survive, even without the Chinese nation," Boon Jin said, stating the principle he would uphold through years and decades ahead. "In America I've seen people who are loyal American citizens, and they keep their Chinese identity. Just as the influence of Greece and Rome has shaped Western civilisation, so Chinese culture can survive wherever our people go, though the Chinese Empire falls."

But Father missed Boon Jin's point, as many people would miss it in future; and he would be attacked by people from both sides who couldn't accept a separation between culture and national loyalty.

"What is this treasonable talk about the fall of the Empire?" Father shouted, standing up. "I will hear no more. What kind of unnatural son are you? Thank heaven I have your brother to keep our family honour. You are a curse to me, not a blessing, you are a disgrace to us, a shame to your ancestors!"

Boon Jin stood up too, looking pale and breathing hard as Father yelled at him.

"You've become a barbarian in the South, bringing back your barbarian wife! You have forgotten all the teaching you were given and turned away from your ancestors; you are a disloyal, unfilial son!" Working himself up to fury, Father hit Boon Jin twice across the face; and glared at him for a minute, and stormed away.

Boon Jin stood paralysed. Quek Choo came and took his arm, he let off some of his feelings by snarling at her.

"Boon Jin, you mustn't make Father angry like that," Mother said nervously.

"I shouldn't have tried to talk to him about politics. He'll never change," Boon Jin said bitterly.

For the rest of their visit Father refused to speak to Boon Jin. He did not feel grateful for the money that Boon Jin had brought home, as he took it for granted that a son should support his parents. He was loyal to the Qing dynasty to the end, and he did not forgive Boon Jin.

# 12

> Man from his beginning was virtuous,
> Later corrupted by evil influence.
> By studying the Classic Books
> Inborn morality may be restored.
>
> —*Attributed to Lu Xiang Shan*
> *16<sup>th</sup> Century*

When Boon Jin returned from China in June he found very gloomy faces at the Chinese Chamber of Commerce. "It's unbelievable," traders muttered in corners. "Impossible." The rubber price was down: in less than a year, it had dropped to one-third of that euphoric twelve-dollar high. Now it was only three dollars and ninety-three cents.

The thousands of acres that had been planted during the rubber-fever period had begun production. That year the total output of rubber was twice what it had been the year before—and the next year it doubled again. The price collapsed. The boom years were over.

Boon Jin's milling factory had to work much harder for its

profits. So he watched with great interest, as Chong Beng's friend from Batu Pahat brought crates of new equipment to the factory and started setting it up.

One day Boon Jin inspected the factory with his foreman, Yin. They walked through the tall building, peering at their machinery in the gloom, hardly noticing the thick rubber smell which they had grown used to.

"Any problems with the work?" Boon Jin asked Yin, raising his voice over the thump of the steam engine and the rattle of the rollers. They were standing near the pile of dirty, contaminated rubber, which a worker was feeding into the first set of rollers. As the scrap was stretched and twisted, twigs and earth and little stones sprang out and showered down from the machine.

Yin told Boon Jin about various things needing attention. Then Boon Jin glanced towards the corner where the man from Batu Pahat had set up his boilers and moulds.

"Is that getting in your way? Is it interfering with your work?" he asked Yin. He didn't want Yin getting upset by the new arrangements.

"I can manage all right," replied Yin, pleased by Boon Jin's concern.

Boon Jin went over to look at the set-up. The operator showed him the first set of rubber boots being taken out of the moulds. On Chong Beng's next visit he took a load of boots which he thought he could sell in Penang and Perak, while some were sent to Columbia-Oriental Traders to be sold in America.

. . .

Chong Beng had been quite subdued since the venture in Canton had failed. But one October morning he came bursting into Boon Jin's house in Katong shouting, "Wuchang has fallen! Wuchang has fallen!"

"Fallen to you people you mean? Dr. Sun's organised another uprising already?"

"Yes, I mean no, I mean Wuchang's been taken by revolutionaries, but not our group of people. Dr. Sun's away in America right now, in fact. But all the same, this is part of his great plan for the renewal and rebirth of China! You know where Wuchang is? Right in the heart of the country, controlling the great river! We must support the men at Wuchang, we mustn't allow them to be defeated."

"Oh well yes, we'll do what we can."

"The Penang headquarters got a cable from our Tong Meng Hui brothers in Wuchang, asking us for financial support. They are counting on us and we must not let them down. I'm giving one thousand of my own money, Boon Jin; do you think the company can make a donation?" Boon Jin agreed, quite carried away by Chong Beng's enthusiasm.

The fighting Nationalists held on successfully to what they had won at Wuchang, on the tenth day of the tenth month of 1911. In several battles they defeated the government forces and spread along the Yangtze River. Day by day the Chinese in the Nanyang got news of the Nationalists' victorious advance. Town after town, province after province, was announced to have been "recovered" from the Manchus, and restored to Han Chinese rule.

The people of Singapore seethed with excitement. Chinatown was full of public rallies and street corner orators. New publications sprang up and flourished. Shiploads of eager volunteers departed for China to join the fighting.

Chong Beng worked very hard, collecting funds to send to the fighters. Although times were difficult, people made great sacrifices. Chong Beng returned to Penang and wrote back that the same kind of thing was happening there: labourers and old serving-women were pressing their life savings into his hands, begging him to send the money to the fighting brothers in China.

• • •

Boon Jin watched the excitement with a kind of detachment, as the final fall of Imperial rule seemed more and more certain. He wasn't sure whether he wished for the revolutionaries to be defeated again. It did not look as though they were going to be.

One morning he got a call at the office on the new telephone. "Mr. Tan Boon Jin? This is the Immigration Officer at Collyer Quay. We have a lady just landed who says she's your mother; could you come along and confirm her identity?"

"I'm coming," Boon Jin said, horrified. He had been trying to keep away his fears for his family, now they all came over him. He called his carriage and tried to hurry to the docks; but the streets were crowded with excited people. He heard a street orator at Hong Lim Green shouting: 'Hear the great news! Hear the great news! Peking has been taken by the glorious revolutionaries! The Emperor has been taken prisoner! Imperial rule has ended and the people are victorious!"

Boon Jin knew the news was important but at that moment he was too anxious to think about it. He hurried into the Immigration Office. His mother got up from a chair and tottered on her bound feet to cling tightly to him.

"Boon Jin! Your father! Your father! Your eldest brother!"

"Where's my father? What's happened?"

"They killed him. Ah, ah, the rebels killed your father!" Mother began to wail. "They shot him in town. They killed Boon Huat. They burned our house. They burned our fields and stole the horses and pigs."

Boon Jin tried to comfort her. She wept loudly and easily. She had had time to get used to the catastrophe. Now she was safe, all her grief came out. "Don't cry, Mother. You will be safe now. Don't cry," Boon Jin said over and over. He felt stunned.

Mother had escaped with his sister-in-law and four servants and a lot of baggage. Boon Jin got them through the Immigration, called a couple of gharries for the servants and baggage and helped the ladies into his carriage to go back to Katong.

The streets were full of excited people. Boon Jin remembered the news of the capture of Peking. Outside a shop someone was putting up a blue and white flag on a flagstaff wreathed in red cloth.

"The rebels carried that flag when they came to burn our house," Mother said. "Our old groom saw it all, he was hiding in the pigsty to see if he could save anything. But they came shouting and singing, they looted the house and took everything of value. They broke up the furniture and threw down our clothing and bed quilts, and set fire to them. They burned the Ancestors' Hall, and the Jade Study with all the books."

The carriage was jammed in a crowd in Kling Street. The people were roaring and cheering. A man was hauling down the flag flying in front of one of the Chinese banks, the dragon flag of the Emperors of China. Two bank officials waited for him, with a little charcoal stove. Someone made a speech. The dragon flag was poked onto the burning coals; when the heavy folds almost choked the fire they were raked up with a stick, and the fire was fanned, and the whole flag burnt.

"We all ran away from the house," Mother said. "When the rebels killed Father and Eldest Brother, we packed our things in a great hurry and went to Amoy. Your two uncles and their families are living there now. I said I wanted to go to my son in the Nanyang, so they helped me find a boat. The journey was terrible, so cramped, so uncomfortable! And while we were in Amoy, old Huang came and told us how the rebels burnt the house."

Boon Jin leaned out and told the driver to go through North Bridge Road instead of the narrower, crowded streets. He sat back and asked the question he was afraid of: "What happened to Father and Brother?"

Mother started weeping again. Father and Brother had gone to Kim Chiam one day to call on Magistrate Pu. The rebel army had attacked the town. The gates were closed and the soldiers tried to defend the walls. The rebels were numerous, and well-armed, and determined.

"We heard the guns firing all day," Mother said. "At evening the shooting stopped and we thought the rebels had gone away. But your Father didn't come home. Next morning our neighbour came and told us that the rebels got into the town. They slaughtered so many, they killed the Magistrate and all his officials. They killed everyone inside the Magistrate's courts."

There was a deafening rattle ahead, a string of explosions. "Guns shooting!" Mother and Sister-in-law shrieked. "The rebels are here!"

"It's firecrackers," the driver called down to them.

The horses backed nervously from the noise. Traffic ahead was stopping as more strings of firecrackers were let off. People in the street were cheering and laughing, and waving the blue and white flags. The carriage was caught in the jammed traffic while the thunder of the firecrackers went on unendingly, and when at last they could proceed the ground was carpeted with the bright debris. North Bridge Road and South Bridge Road were crimson as though the streets were flooded with blood.

. . .

It was a lie, Boon Jin found out later. It wasn't true, in early November, that Peking fell to the rebels and the Emperor was captured: but the false rumour had the Chinese in Singapore believing that victory was won, the old age was dead and the new day had come.

There were rallies all over Singapore and Malaya at which people by the hundreds cut off their queues. Rich merchants who had been favourites of the Qing Government cut their hair and promised to support the new revolution: and whether their conversion was due to prudence or to real republican spirit, it showed that in the minds of the most pragmatic, there was no more future in supporting the Imperial Government.

The fall of Peking was an imaginary event, that was more powerful than the truth. The story made people dismantle the loyalties and thought habits of a lifetime; and when that period of rejoicing ended, the Empire of China was a ghost that had no more power over the minds of its people.

• • •

On the fifteenth of December Dr. Sun Yat Sen arrived in Singapore. He was on his way back to China, to be made President of the new Republic of China. This time he did not quietly creep to some safe house: a huge cheering crowd went to the docks to meet him, and all the prominent people went on board to shake his hand.

He had, after all, fought no blow in the final battle for liberation—he had been in America during the Wuchang Rising. Now he was seen not so much as a wild rebel as a wise man, a prophet; they were already calling him the Father of the Republic.

Every Chinese in Singapore seemed to have been caught up in a rush of pride and patriotism. Old enmities were forgotten. The Straits Chinese Association gave a great dinner for Dr. Sun, at a prominent member's house in Pasir Panjang. Khoo Tiong Lay was there, proudly claiming leadership of the Singapore Tong Meng Hui.

Dr. Lim Boon Keng was not there: no one ever knew how quick he might have been to salute the new Republic, for he was still in Europe, still on his mission for the honour of the Dragon flag.

Boon Jin was not at any of the celebrations. His father's death gave him good reason not to go. He seemed to be the only person in Singapore who felt regret that more than two thousand years of China's history had been swept away.

• • •

Late at night Boon Jin left his room and went out to an upstairs balcony of his house. He could hear the murmur of the sea on Katong beach under the stars. He paced up and down in the cool dark.

Quek Choo came out to join him. "What's the matter, can't you sleep? I've brought you some tea. What's on your mind, won't you tell me?"

Boon Jin had never expected his wife to share his deepest pains and troubles. But Quek Choo coaxed him to find words for his unrest.

"Our home was burned," he said, gazing out into the night. "Our Jade Study was burned. Our Ancestors' Hall was burned, with all the tablets. I keep seeing the ashes and black timbers in my mind. I think of my father and my brother. I've made offerings so that their spirits will be happy, but I don't know what happened to their bones."

"One day we'll go back and look for their graves," Quek Choo said.

"I will never go back to China," Boon Jin said, with sorrow and determination. "Not while it is ruled by the men who killed my family."

Quek Choo gently touched Boon Jin's arm. He felt her unspoken sympathy. He turned round and stared at her unhappily.

"Quek Choo, I keep thinking about how my father was loyal to the Emperor, till the moment he died. He thought I was a disloyal son. My duty was to have stayed with him in China, not to run away."

"But he sent you away—your duty was to obey him."

"If I had been the kind of son he wanted me to be, I would have been with Boon Huat beside him, when the rebels came."

"Then you would have been killed too."

"So I'm alive because I was an undutiful son!"

"You're punishing yourself for nothing, Boon Jin," Quek Choo said firmly. "You couldn't have saved your father and brother. It's better after all that you're alive, to preserve the family name and traditions. You told me once—what were those words, that your ancestor wrote on the wall of the Jade Study?"

"Yes. 'Wen shueh ming guan'," Boon Jin said in Mandarin. " 'Classic learning, bright light'. It means that study of the

Classics brings enlightenment to people's minds. If all Chinese had known and loved the teachings of Confucius, we might still have an Emperor."

"Emperor or no Emperor, it's still worth preserving the teachings of Confucius, isn't it?"

"Certainly. But I think the Nationalists will not preserve them. We shall lose yet more of the past, if study of the Classics dies out!"

"Well, you must stop that happening, Boon Jin!"

"What do you think I could do?" Boon Jin looked up with new interest.

"You might start a school in Singapore perhaps…"

"A special institution, to keep the old scholarship alive—to preserve and extend Confucian studies! I could try to get enough people interested, to collect funds and open a new school!"

"Yes, do that," said Quek Choo. "I am sure your father's spirit would approve."

That night Boon Jin and Quek Choo planned the school for advanced Chinese studies, which one day became Wenguang Academy. They discussed how it would try to integrate the old learning with the new. They laid down the principles which would continue to guide their work for years to come; they talked for hours, and Boon Jin put aside his guilt and regrets.

. . .

Dawn was breaking over the sea when they went to bed. Boon Jin slept peacefully with his arm around Quek Choo.

He dreamt that he stood on a green hill, among old blackened timbers half-buried in the earth. Along the hillside a small boy came scampering, calling to another child in a yellow coat. They ran happy and unafraid, over grass and tiny flowers growing between the quiet ruins.

The children played along the old paths of a forgotten garden. The light of a clear spring morning in China shone around them. They laughed and chased butterflies down to the river bank, and their high voices floated back when they were gone from sight.

IN A HOUSE in Siglap, a well-known architect proudly points to a large photograph in a heavy silver frame.

"This photo was taken in 1920," he says, "on the inaugural day of the Wenguang Academy. That's my grandfather, the founder. On his right stands Dr. Lim Boon Keng, the Academy's first patron, the man who was the most influential Singaporean of his time. No, I don't know much about Dr. Lim's involvement in China. What he did here was much more important. He was given a medal, the Order of the British Empire, for his work in Singapore."

"Standing on the other side, in Chinese Army uniform, that's my grandmother's brother. Years later, he was killed fighting the Japanese in Manchuria. And next to him is my grandmother. She helped my grandfather in all his efforts to establish the Academy, and build it up to what it is now. They were remarkable people."

Boon Jin and Quek Choo gaze out of the photograph at their descendants.

"Man's existence is impermanent, but Heaven and earth

exist for ever; I remember my grandfather saying that," the architect reflects. "There are some eternal and unchanging truths, he said, and in our new society we should hold onto them still."